Ambivalent Souls

ALSO FROM POETS & TRAITORS PRESS

Advances in Embroidery by Ahmad Al-Ashqar
Relative Genitive by Val Vinokur
Education by Windows by Johnny Lorenz
A Life Replaced by Olga Livshin
Other Shepherds by Nina Kossman

Ambivalent Souls

Robert E. Tanner

a true translation of Alexander Pushkin's
'Eugene Onegin'

Stanza 8.XI first appeared in *Blue Dolphin* as "A Thought on Youth."

Cover image: Alexander Pushkin

Published 2022 in New York by Poets & Traitors Press
www.poets-traitors.com
poetstraitors@gmail.com

Editors: Val Vinokur, Mia Perez, Julia Curl
Guest Editor: Peter Scotto

Published in the United States of America.

Poets & Traitors Press is an independent publisher of books of poetry and translations by a single author/translator. The press emerged from the Poet/Translator Reading Series and from the New School's Literary Translation Workshop to showcase authors who travel between writing and translation, artists for whom Language is made manifest through languages and whose own word carries, shapes, and is shaped by that of another.

Poets & Traitors Press acknowledges support from Eugene Lang College, the New School Bachelor's Program for Adults and Transfer Students, and the New School Foreign Languages Department.

ISBN: 978-0-9990737-5-9

To the people of Ukraine,
Where hope still lives

Ambivalent Souls

CONTENTS

FOREWORD

Habent sua fata libelli. My "Poltava" was not a success. No doubt, it didn't deserve it.

—Alexander Pushkin,
"Ripostes to the Critics of Poltava" (1830)

Pro captu lectoris, habent sua fata libelli. "According to the capacities of the reader, books have their fate." The fate, the doom, the destiny of the little book you hold in your hands is inextricably bound up with the circumstances of its coming together, and with the capacities with which you read it.

In 2018, after he graduated from an MFA pogram, Robert Tanner, an American poet and writer, travelled to Ukraine with the Peace Corps to teach English and learn Russian. Why learn Russian in Ukraine? Why not Ukraine? Since both Russian and Ukrainian are deeply woven into the linguistic fabric of that place, he found any number of generous and knowledgeable tutors willing to help. Moreover, for someone like Tanner, interested as he was in Russian literature, it seemed a logical choice. Writers who made permanent contributions to writing in Russian, writers without whom that thing we call Russian literature as we know it cannot be conceived—Nikolai Gogol, Mikhail Bulgakov, Mikhail Zoshchenko, Isaac Babel, Yury Olesha to name a few—every one of them got their start somewhere in that place we call Ukraine.

And there, in Ukraine, Tanner falls in love. Prompted by students who recite the poet's verse to him, encouraged by his tutors, he falls in love with Pushkin—and, it seems, with a woman named Nadezdha (Hope), who shares her name with Pushkin's mother. He wonders about the statues of Pushkin he encounters on the squares of Ukrainian towns; and he then makes what will turn out to be a fatal decision: he decides to translate *Eugene Onegin* in its entirety into English in meter and rhyme. This is, to say the least, remarkable. To put 5541 lines of Pushkin's fast-moving iambic tetrameter into English verse; to reproduce in the short-winded monosyllables, disyllables and trisyllables of English the demanding yet infinitely adaptable Onegin stanza (aBaBccDDeFFeGG) which gets its aesthetic charge from Russian's free-flowing polysyllables — that would be a challenge even for the most experienced translators. (Vladimir Nabokov gave up and damned anyone who would try.) However for a translator relatively new to Russian (like Tanner), this is audacious, if not insane on its face. Then, setting about his work, he makes an even more consequential decision: into the interstices of the text, into the dropped lines and the cancelled stanzas that are a structural feature of Pushkin's novel, into the metrical spaces opened up by translating long Russian words into short English ones, he will write himself and the story of this translation.

In doing so, he is following Pushkin's lead: into a simple story line (in Viktor Shklovsky's formulation "When A loves B, B rejects A; When B loves, A rejects B") Pushkin inserts digressions, observations, meditations, asides, bio-bibliographical commentary, and even a stanza or two where he meets up with his hero on the embankment of the Neva, so that the poet (or "Poet" for the critically fastidious) becomes as much or more of a presence in this work as any of his four main characters (Onegin, Tatiana, Olga, Lensky).

* * *

The road for guns and tanks has always been paved by books.
–Oksana Zabuzhko,
Times Literary Supplement (April 2022)

In the wake of the horror unleashed on Ukraine by Russia beginning February 24, 2022, the world that gave birth to this translation has vanished, at least for the foreseeable future. The colossal Soviet era-monument to "Russian-Ukrainian

Friendship" in Kiev (c. 1982) has been dismantled. According to reports, streets or squares named in honor of Russian writers (and even Ukrainian writers who wrote in Russian) will be renamed. In Ternopil, along with a monument to cosmonaut Yury Gagarin ("the first man in space"), the monument to Alexander Pushkin (built in the 1960s like Gagarin's) has been demolished. According to reports, Russian shelling has destroyed a museum dedicated to philosopher and poet, Hryhoriy Skovoroda in eastern Ukraine.

If it is indeed true that, as Ukrainian writer Oksana Zabuzhko maintains, "it was Russian literature that wove the camouflage net for Russia's tanks," then Pushkin, as its founder, may well deserve whatever he gets. Is he part of a longstanding Russian colonial project, the emptying of Ukrainian cultural space as part of a "rhetorical preparation for destroying it" (Timothy Snyder)? If so, should we "take a long hard look at our bookshelves" (Zabuzhko again) and purge Pushkin, or at least demote him?

Even the poet's most ardent admirers would find themselves hard pressed to defend Pushkin's politics. "To the Slanderers of Russia" (1831) alone is enough to damn him. A snarling defense of Russia's brutal suppression of the Polish uprising of 1830 against its European critics, the poem anticipates Putin's fulminations in his now infamous essay "On the Historical Unity of Russians and Ukrainians." Pushkin warns Russia's detractors in Europe to keep their opinions to themselves because 1) Russia saved Europe from Tyranny in the past (Napoleon in this case) 2) the conflict between Poland and Russia is an inter-Slavic family affair that they have never really understood anyway. He concludes on a note of menace that now sounds all-too familiar:

You're very big on words – just you go ahead and try it!
Or perhaps you think the warrior of old is just resting on his laurels,

Without the strength to fix the bayonet that beat the Turks at Izmail?
Or the word of Russia's Tsar has somehow lost its power?
Or tangling it up with Europe is something new for us?
Or Russians may have lost their taste for victory?
Or that we're too few? That from Perm to the Crimea,
From the Finland's frozen cliffs to Georgia's fiery coast,
From the Kremlin's battered walls,
To the walls of immobile China,
With gleam of cold-steel bristling,
The Russian land will not rise up against you?
So go ahead, you loudmouths, go ahead,
You send your envenomed sons:
There's a place for them in Russia's fields,
Among the graves of those who came before them.

Moreover, in a narrative poem written the year before, Pushkin celebrates Peter the Great's decisive victory at Poltava over Charles XII of Sweden and Cossack hetman Ivan Mazepa, his rebellious Ukrainian ally (1709). Worse, he depicts Mazepa, now a Ukrainian national hero whose image adorns the 10-hryvna banknote, as a criminal, a traitor and a coward. Peter's victory not only gave Pushkin's poem its title, it secured Russia's place as hegemon in Eastern Europe and a ruler of Ukraine for the next several centuries. Sir Edward Creasy included the battle in his Victorian-era classic The Fifteen Decisive Battles of the World (1851) "on account of what it overthrew as well as for what it established," i.e. Russian military might and thereby Imperial Russia as a player in the age of European Empire.

When Pushkin imagines his posthumous fame in his great "Monument" of 1836, he imagines the reach of his immortality expanding outwards with the expanse of Russian imperial dominion:

Word of me will make its way through all of Greater Russia
And every tribe and tongue will call me by my name
Proud grandsons of the Slavs, the Finn, the Tungus,
Yet untamed, and friend of the steppe, the Kalmyk.
Those "proud grandsons of the Slavs" certainly include "Little

Russians" (Ukrainians) "White Russians" and maybe even Poles, while the others (Tungus, Finn and Kalmyk) stand for all subject peoples to the East and to the North.

Rhetorical camouflage netting in iambics?

* * *

Pushkin is our all.

—Apollon Grigoriev (1859)

Because of the sheer magnitude of his poetic achievement, Pushkin has been regularly pressed into service for causes other than his own. With the unveiling of the Pushkin monument in Moscow in 1881—at which Dostoevsky gave his famous speech about Russia's "universality attained not by the sword, but by the force of brotherhood and of our brotherly striving toward the reunification of mankind"—Pushkin becomes the "Official Poet of the Russian Intelligentsia." In 1899, on the hundredth anniversary of this birth, he was made the "Official Poet of Tsarist Russia" (when you could purchase "Pushkin Kugels" among the vast array of Pushkin-themed merchandise being offered for sale). On the hundredth anniversary of his death in 1937, he was transformed once again into "The Official Poet of the Soviet Union", but not before the Russian diaspora ("Russia Abroad") in a countermove declares his birthday "The Day of Russian Culture." For the diaspora, Pushkin became the embodiment of the true Russian values the Emigration had sworn to protect against those of an inauthentic Bolshevized Russia.

Now what? "Pushkin the Official Poet of Empire"? "Pushkin the Official Poet of Russian Revanchist Colonialism"?

No matter how politically relevant, or morally compelling it is to frame Pushkin as a literary precursor of Putinism might seem under the current circumstances, it is, like all attempts to contain him, inadequate.

* * *

All he ever taught was – Might.

—Marina Tsvetaeva,
"Poems to Pushkin" (1931)

Marina Tsvetaeva makes precisely this point in a cycle of densely allusive, highly polemical, and characteristically elliptical poems written in 1931 and first published in Paris in time for the jubilee year of 1937. Tsvetaeva, who had suffered at the hands of conservative critics who deployed Pushkin as a club to cudgel her innovative poetic practice, rejects any and all attempts to monumentalize, compartmentalize, canonize, institutionalize, nationalize or otherwise domesticate him in any terms that diminish the explosive power of his transgressive creativity:

> Scourge of gendarmes, god of students,
> Gall for husbands, fun for wives –
> Pushkin as a monument?
> Cast as his Stone Guest? Him –
>
> Impudent, unmannerly
> Pushkin – Guardian of Virtue?
>
> Critic (whining), whiner (likewise):
> "Oh where (big sob) is Pushkin's vaunted
> Sense of measure?" Maybe you forget
> His sense of seawaves
> Beating hard against the granite?
>
> Him, that salty seawave Pushkin
> Cast in role of dictionary? [...]
>
> You can't cover up what's Black

With White — not even worth a try!
So where's your Famous Russian Classic,
Who called the African sky —

His own, the river Neva — rot.
Pushkin — Russian Patriot?   [...]

Tsvetaeva's Pushkin is radically uncanonizable. He never sets
limits for poetic creativity, but is always the embodiment of an
unbounded and unbindable liberating energy that transcends
time or place:

> Overcoming
> Russian inertia:
> Pushkin's Genius?
> Pushkin's muscle!
>
> On the deadweight
> Whale of fate:
> Muscle of flying
> Of racing
> Of fight. [...]
>
> Someone who bore him off on his bier:
> "Muscle like an
> Athlete
> Not like a poet."
>
> That was: the strength
> Of the seraphim
> The indestructible muscle
> Of wing.

It can be argued that Tsvetaeva's Pushkin is "subjective" or even
that she "makes Pushkin into something he isn't." That is as it may

be. However, like other great writers, Pushkin seemed to have an uncanny knack for predicting the terms of his own posthumous fame. In the very same "Monument" in which he imagines his glory expanding to fill imperial space, he imagines his continued life to be bound up with his life in the hearts, minds, and ears of poets coming after him. And it doesn't take an empire; all it takes is one:

> No, not all of me will die. My soul in cherished lyre
> Will long outlive my dust and so escape decay—
> And I will be renowned down in this world
> As long as there still lives a single poet.

Thus, Robert Tanner, gentleman from New Orleans, teaching English and learning Russian in Ukraine, found Pushkin, and he responded with this translation. Obligated, like any translator, to know what the original says, but like any good translator, never bound by it, he audaciously writes himself into Pushkin's text, and far from making Pushkin into something he isn't, he makes Pushkin into something he is.

* * *

So, dear reader, carus lector, the fate of this little book now rests in your hands, in your capacity to read, to listen, to hear and respond to something you may not have expected, but is well worth your attention and your sympathy.

Peter Scotto
South Hadley, Massachusetts
May 10, 2022

1799 - 1837   ALEXANDER PUSHKIN
Pushkin and Onegin, in a letter to L. Pushkin, 1824

18

Ambivalent Souls

DEDICATION

Pétri de vanité il avait encore plus de cette espèce d'orgueil qui fait avouer
avec la même indifférence les bonnes comme les mauvaises actions, suite d'un
sentiment de supériorité peut-être imaginaire.

—Tiré d'une lettre particuliére.*

Indifferent to the smug world's pleasure,
I'd rather have a friend's review
and wish I could present a treasure,
a tribute worthier of you,
more worthy of your spirit's splendor
and the devoted dream it wreathes,
a work both lofty and most tender,
with limpid poetry that breathes.
But so it is. Indulge this slender
novel comprised of motley verse,
half humorous, half melancholy,
of simple folk and ideal's folly,
an offhand fruit of *time adverse*,
of sleepless nights, light inspirations,
my unripe and my withered years,
of intellect's cold observations
and the heart's notes, oft soaked in tears.

---

* Puffed up with vanity, he had still more of the kind of pride that made him
admit, with equal indifference, to good as well as bad actions, a result of a feeling
of—perhaps imaginary—superiority.

—Pulled from a private letter.

CHAPTER ONE

И жить торопится и чувствовать спешит.
—Кн. Вяземский*

1.I
"My uncle is a man of honor,
and he insisted on esteem
when he—not kidding—was a goner;
you can't invent a better scheme.
Let others learn from his example,
but, God, the tedium is ample:
attending him both night and day,
to sit and never step away!
What treachery to act so badly,
to entertain the mostly-dead,
to fluff the pillows on his bed,
to offer medicine so sadly,
to sigh and tell yourself *again*,
the Deuce will take you soon—but when!"

1.II
So thought a youngish rake while daring
to hasten post through dusty air,
with fearsome Zeus's will declaring
the youth his family's only heir.
Dear *Ruslan and Ludmila* lovers!
My hero here, between these covers,
right now, without yet more ado,
I'd like to introduce to you:
Onegin, a good friend most splendid,
was born upon the Neva's shores,
a birthplace maybe also yours,
or, reader, where your star ascended.
I sometimes strolled upon that bank,
but now—for me—the north is rank.

* Impatient to live as quick to feel. —Prince Vyazemsky

1.III
Throughout his brilliant, noble service,
his dad thrice yearly gave a ball.
With debts the man was never nervous,
and by the end he'd squandered all.
Eugene was under fate's protection:
at first it was *Madame's* inspection,
and then *Monsieur* did her unseat.
The child was boisterous but sweet.
Monsieur l'Abbé, a poor French creature,
so not to tire the little one,
would teach him everything in fun
and, since he was no dreary preacher,
would gently chide his pranks with talk
and then a Summer Garden walk.

1.IV
And when the age of young defiance,
the age of hopes and tender woe,
did reach and shake Eugene's compliance,
Monsieur was told he'd have to go.
Behold Onegin's liberation:
sporting a London fop's creation,
his coif precisely *à la mode*,
into society he strode.
His French was thoroughly perfected
for self-expression and the pen.
He danced a deft mazurka, then
his bow was simple, unaffected.
What more would you? The social sphere
declared him bright and quite the dear.

1.V
We all endured some education,
although the hows and whats aren't clear,
so, God bless, *any* cultivation
did sparkle wondrous in our sphere.
Onegin was, in view of many

(strict judges not excusing any),
a cultured but pedantic gent.
He had a lucky social bent
for touching in his conversations
most everything without prepare,
showing an expert's learnèd air
by keeping mum in disputations,
and rousing ladies' smiles with sparks
from startling, humorous remarks.

1.VI
Now Latin's fallen out of favor,
and yet, to tell the truth, he knew
the Roman tongue enough to savor
a *vale* rather than adieu.
He could dissect most Latin phrases,
interpret Juvenal to praises,
and could recall—almost, it's true—
some Virgil—well, a verse or two.
He fully lacked the inclination
to rummage antiquated dust
(by annals, he remained nonplussed),
but anecdotes without citation,
from Romulus to present day,
he could from memory relay.

1.VII
He lacked the lofty love for lyrics
to sacrifice his life for sound.
He couldn't iambs tell from pyrrhics,
no matter how we would expound.
Theocritus and Homer? Never!
His Adam Smith he read, however,
and economics he knew well.
That is, he could with judgment tell
how to enrich and build a nation
and what it lives upon, and why
it does not need a gold supply:

one *simple product* is salvation.
His father couldn't understand
and fully mortgaged all his land.

1.VIII
As for the rest of Eugene's learning,
I lack the leisure to run through.
But what his genius was concerning,
what more than all the arts he knew,
what was for him from adolescence
a work, a pain, a pleasing essence,
what kept his melancholy suaged
and day-long laziness engaged—
this was the art of tender passion
about which Ovid sang with praise,
for which his bright rebellious days
would end in suffering, out of fashion,
in poor Moldova, far from Rome,
on a wild steppe so unlike home.

1.IX
And here our Pushkin cut a stanza,
which said that we learn love from lit.
(Nabokov's gloss is a bonanza,
but his translation I'd omit.)
I should explain sesquipedalian
expressions aren't—in Russian—alien.
Eight syllables from Pushkin's quill
I must, in English, bloat to fill:
"May I present," becomes, from Russian,
"I'd like to introduce to you..."
your translator: an expat, *too*.
(To clarify the short discussion
on what those lines on Ovid mean,
that's Pushkin's exile.) Now Eugene!

1.X
How early could Eugene dissemble,

conceal a hope or—jealous—vent,
instill a trust then make it tremble,
appear depressed, truly lament,
present himself as proud, submissive,
considerate or quite dismissive!
How calm his silent elegance,
how ardent was his eloquence
in heartfelt notes, how unaffected!
In breathing one thing, loving it,
oh, how he could himself forget!
His glance was tender, unexpected,
now shy, now bold, at times, while here
it shines with a submissive tear!

1.XI
How he could give a new impression,
or innocence in fun amaze,
or menace with a primed depression,
or, to amuse, pleasantly praise,
or snatch a moment of devotion,
or, using wits and his emotion,
vanquish a virgin prejudice,
await unwilling tenderness,
entreat, demand a declaration,
then overhear the heart's first throes
—pursuing love our Pushkin knows—
and sudden gain an assignation...
and afterward, alone with her,
give lessons that the censors blur!

1.XII
How early was Eugene's arrival,
soon troubling hearts of staunch coquettes!
And when he wished to crush a rival,
he'd spread such scandalous vignettes!
What spiteful snares he would get ready!
But you, you blessèd husbands, said he
remained a friend who could engross.

The crafty husband keeps him close.
(We know he should have kept him closer,
this poor, devoted Faublas fan,
who yet admires the ladies' man.)
The hoary husband cautions "whoa, sir,"
while the grand cuckold beams his pride
in self and lunch and blushing bride.

> 1.XIII
> Then Pushkin cut the next two verses,
> about Eugene seducing lambs:
> young widows he never coerces
> but beds with shocking epigrams.
> (One pictures Pushkin in such places.)
> A tomcat or a wolf, he chases
> lethargically then all at once.
> I can't endure these carnal hunts.
> Yet the first verse of my translation,
> when read one cold December night,
> lacked shocks, indeed, but did delight
> and was, I guess, my own flirtation.
> His verse attracts, it must be said:
> it turned a lovely woman's head.
>
> 1.XIV
> Near Pushkin's exile in Odessa,
> I'm volunteering in Ukraine.
> I teach some English and address a
> poetic need. Let me explain.
> In every town (whose names I garble),
> I'd mark a street or park or marble
> to Pushkin. Still, I wasn't sold
> till one dull Monday morn I told
> my class my weekend occupation—
> Tatiana's letter, chapter three—
> and they recited it to me!
> Despite many a fine translation,
> to us *Onegin's* nigh unknown,
> and so I offer you my own.

1.XV
Would be, the morning bird was singing,
when little notes his help would leave.
And? Invitations they were bringing.
Three parties want him for the eve:
a ball, kid's bash and celebration
that Pushkin skips in this summation.
Where did my prankster gallop first?
The town is easily traversed.
He'd make them all, so for the present,
Onegin wore his morning dress—
and *bolivar*, donned to impress.
He strolled the boulevard so pleasant,
until his watchful Breguet'd spring.
Its dinner bell then did its thing.

1.XVI
"Make way! Make way!" his man would holler.
Already dark, by sleigh he flew,
frost silvering his beaver collar.
He rushed to Talon's, as he knew
Kaverin—Pushkin's friend—was waiting.
He entered. Corks popped, liberating
a gushing flow of Comet Wine
(1811 vintage, fine,
and named for that celestial body
next seen in *War and Peace*). His nosh:
roast-beef *sanglant* and truffles posh,
what French cuisine did best embody,
and deathless Strasbourg pie they'd squeeze
tween pineapples and living cheese.

1.XVII
His thirst requests more wine, libations
to quench the scorching fat filet,
but Breguet's tintinnabulations
announce the start of the ballet.
Our tyrant of the stage is vicious,

his zest for actresses—capricious.
An honorary citizen
of backstage life, Eugene is in
quick flight to the night's presentation,
where, breathing privilege (freedom's flaw),
each gives applause to *entrechats*,
and Cleopatra—hissed damnation.
Moena, though (who history's blurred),
he hails—just so his voice is heard.

1.XVIII
Here Pushkin pauses to remember.
In these two stanzas added late,
he talks of times he was a member
of the theatrical estate.
Slight Russian playwrights we've forgotten
(Fonvizin, Ozerov—who brought in
the star Semyonova to share
the tears, applause, and spotlight's stare)
and Didelot, doyen of dances,
win Pushkin's praises. Shakhovskoy,
whose own Moena hoi polloi
just hailed last verse, our bard advances
because he knew, Nabokov smirks,
the man would soon adapt his works.

1.XIX
My angels! (Pushkin reminisces.)
Oh, where are you? Such joy! Such rue!
Are you the same? Did different misses
succeed—without replacing—you?
And will I hear again your chorus?
Or see a friendly face before us?
And will I see a soulful soar,
a leap by Russia's Terpsichore?
(My childhood in New Orleans taught me

the street before the muse, I fret.)
Will, disenchanted, my lorgnette
discover all the world's forgot me?
Will I inaudibly then yawn
and think about the times long gone?

1.XX
The house is full. The boxes shimmer.
Parterre and orchestra—a crush.
The gallery's a restless simmer.
The curtain rises with a hush.
Here half ethereal, resplendent,
the magical baton's attendant,
amidst a thronging nymphet sea
is poised Istomina. (And she
danced Didelot's famed adaptation,
so Pushkin flatters.) From the floor,
one foot held high, she springs to soar,
a feather swept by inspiration,
her twisted torso now goes straight.
One little foot flicks at its mate.

1.XXI
All clap. (And after hours of striving
to rhyme "he enters," now I *shove*
Onegin through the door.) Arriving,
he aims his opera glass above,
at tiers of unfamiliar graces.
He tramples toes. He looks at faces.
He's horribly dissatisfied,
but bowed to men on every side.
He yawned—ballets he'd seen so many—
then cast a glance towards the stage
and thought it time to turn life's page.
Of Didelot he has had plenty.
But note ambitious Pushkin's clear
that Didelot has no French peer.

1.XXII
Still on the stage to dance caprices
are cupids, devils—dragons too.
Still at the entrance, on pelisses,
exhausted footmen sleep right through.
Still people have not ceased their shuffling,
or clapping, hissing, coughing, snuffling.
(Remark this theme of lists returns
in name-days, dreams, when Tanya yearns.)
Still lights are shining, coachmen swearing,
around the fires they beat their hands.
Still horses fidget at their stands.
But home, to change, Eugene is tearing.
(Our Pushkin wrote this in Ukraine,
where still my heart and love remain.

1.XXIII
Now I've just been evacuated—
so that detail's been on my mind.)
Shall I—so Pushkin contemplated—
depict in truth the very kind
of cabinet where a fashion's pupil
will dress and dress again sans scruple?
All to capricious clientele
that London haberdashers sell
and bring beyond the Baltic breakers
to forests crossed by icy mile,
and all that picky Paris style
designs for luxe, for fashion's takers—
all trimmed the cabinet of Eugene,
philosopher of just eighteen.

1.XXIV
Here's amber in long pipes from fables
from Tsaregrad (now Istanbul).
Here's porcelain and bronze on tables,
and scent here fills a cut-glass jewel.
Such pleasure for his pampered senses!

Combs, files, the list herein commences,
and pairs of scissors—straight and curved.
By thirty brushes was he served.
Rousseau, I should remark in passing,
could not believe that pompous Grimm
dared clean his nails in front of him!

the champ of rights in this ain't right.

1.XXV
A gentleman can be pragmatic
and judge the beauty of his nails.
Our social customs are dogmatic—
why argue when the age prevails?
Thus fearing jealous condemnation,
Eugene, Chadayev's imitation,
(a name only a Slavist knows),
was quite pedantic with his clothes
and was what we once dubbed a dandy.
Three hours before the mirror he'd groom,
and when he left his dressing room,
he looked so good, delish, like candy,
like Venus as a man arrayed,
now dolled up for a masquerade.

1.XXVI
With glimpsing a toilette of fashion,
your curiosity's addressed,
while for an audience of passion,
I could describe here how he dressed.
The plan is risky—a transgression—
yet to describe is my profession.
But *frock*, *gilet*, and *pantaloons*
are foreign words, where Russian swoons.
And now I see—I must acknowledge—
my writing style, already weak,
denied exotics turns quite bleak,

although when young, perhaps in college,
I'd leaf through the *Academy,*
Great Catherine's Russian O.E.D.

1.XXVII
Right now this theme is not convenient,
for we are rushing to a ball,
and my Eugene was never lenient
in urging cabbies—not at all!
Before the winter's darkening houses
lined up in rows—the quarter drowses—
the double lanterns of the hack
pour merry light upon the track
and rainbows on the snowy rises.
Dotted with little lamps around,
the shining mansion will astound.
Through picture glass he recognizes
the profiles flashing past: the poise
of ladies and their glamour boys.

1.XXVIII
Here our protagonist alighted.
An arrow past the porter, he
flew up the marble steps and righted
his hair before the ball's esprit.
The hall is full, musicians weary.
Mazurkas occupy the cheery.
Spurs jangle on a cavalier
(who'll wreck upholstery with that gear!
And, please, remember this for later).
The feet of lovely ladies fly.
Their footsteps captivate the eye
of every fervid ballroom satyr,
while violin swells smother this:
the stylish women's jealous hiss.

1.XXIX
In days of laughter and obsession,

my nights to balls I would devote:
no better place for a confession
or for the passing of a note.
O husbands of good reputation!
I offer my consideration
and ask that you attend with care:
I'm warning you. Beware. Beware!
You, also, mommies, should be keeping
a stricter eye on your young girls.
Adjust your glasses, clutch your pearls!
Or else...or else I fear your weeping!
(Here Pushkin fibs, so it appears,
and says he hasn't sinned in years!)

1.XXX
And I, laments our Pushkin, wasted
so much of my young life on fun!
Alas! Had morals I not tasted,
I'd still love balls, delights begun.
I love the crush, mad youth, flirtations,
splendor, sartorial creations
on women and... I love their feet
(or legs—for Russian lacks discrete
expressions. Really. And in folly
I wonder, where did Pushkin stare
when claiming but three shapely pair
in all of Russia?) Melancholy,
cool, he remembers yet each one,
and in his dreams his heart's undone.

1.XXXI
Now one aside—be patient. Legs I'll
get back to momentarily.
Our Pushkin, feeling here his exile
from Petersburg to the Black Sea,
whence I fled the coronavirus,
mulls deserts, wilds, as if desirous
of thus forgetting little feet:

O feet! Where are you now? Your fleet
and tiny paces left no traces
on melancholy, northern snow.
I spurned for you—how long ago?—
my thirst for fame, my country's graces.
The joys of youth have disappeared,
like footsteps in a meadow cleared.

1.XXXII
Diana's breast, the cheeks of Flora
are, yes, delightful, dearest friends!
Terpsichore, though, has an aura.
Her little foot—for me—transcends.
For with the briefest glimpse foretelling
a quite inestimable swelling
(though prudish Pushkin writes "reward"),
each foot—each leg—so much adored
attracts a willful swarm of yearning.
I love them in spring meadow grass,
on ball parquets that shine like glass,
on winter hobs with firewood burning,
still in Odessa, Pushkin moans,
and seaside, here, on granite stones.

1.XXXIII
When sea awaits a storm's transgression,
how I would envy every wave.
They run, recall, in rough succession
to lie down at the feet they crave!
How I desired to join the breakers
to kiss—for me—those moneymakers!
(Still scholars' guesses aren't complete:
who owned those little, sandy feet?!)
No, never did I feel such anguish
in hungering to kiss young lips,
or cheeks aflame, or fingertips,
or bosoms that forever languish.
No, never did young lust impart
such a dissevering of my heart!

1.XXXIV
Now I recall another story!
Sometimes in cherished dreams I hold
a stirrup, and I feel my quarry
in my two hands. (Here Pushkin sold
no soulless boot, but *foot's* temptation.)
Again seethes my imagination.
Again their touch makes my heart quake,
again the love, again the ache!...
Enough of making reputations!
(Ironic, since we lack their names.)
These haughty ladies have no claims
to love or lyric inspirations.
These charmers' words and looks entreat
deceptively...like legs? No, feet.

1.XXXV
And our Onegin? Done carousing,
our hero drives from ball to bed,
but hustling Petersburg is rousing.
And Pushkin here resumes, it's said,
his total Russian inventory,
like *Moby-Dick* or Hugo's story.
The seller's up, the peddler's gone,
the cabbies line up right at dawn.
Now crunching snow, the milkmaid hurries.
The morning bustles, shutters part,
and columns of blue smoke now start
from chimneys, too. The baker scurries:
the German's prompt in cotton cap.
His bakery's hatch proceeds to flap.

1.XXXVI
But, from the noisy ball so weary
and having turned his morn to night,
lies sleeping peacefully, the dearie,
this child of leisure and delight.
Past noon he will at last awaken,

has plans till dawn, lest I'm mistaken.
Tomorrow is like yesterday,
his life a bit like Groundhog Day.
But was Eugene really contented
with freedom in his youthful bloom,
with glittering conquest, I assume,
with the pleasures each day presented?
Would my Eugene thus vainly feast—
rashly, yet healthy as a beast?

1.XXXVII
No. Soon he ceased being enraptured.
He grew bored with the social scene.
For ages beauties hadn't captured
the wonted thoughts of our Eugene.
Adultery became annoying,
and friends and friendship—past enjoying,
because he couldn't always slake
his thirst from Strasbourg pie and steak
with the champagne that was in fashion,
nor always spew a pointed curse
when his poor head was feeling worse.
And even though a rake of passion,
he swore off strife and finally shed
his love for saber and the lead.

1.XXXVIII
My dear Eugene's historic ailment
("historic," since, year after year,
keen scholars searched for its entailment
despite our Pushkin's being clear)
was "spleen," an Englishman's expression.
That which we Russians call "depression"
had slowly, surely, taken hold.
And while to life he'd grown quite cold,
to shoot himself he lacked the humor.
Like *Childe Harold*, he'd show his gloom
and languor in a drawing room.

Not loving glance nor tasty rumor,
not tactless sigh nor cards misdealt,
he nothing noticed, nothing felt.

1.XXXIX

It first seems Pushkin takes a breather:
three stanzas that do not exist
in draft or in fair copy, either.
His soul and history persist
in characters exemplifying
drinking, despair, a duel, his dying.
And since our Pushkin's final breath,
Onegin's shared his storied death:
in short, his stunning wife's insulted,
whether by will or by caprice,
and jealousy allowed no peace,
so, yes, a fateful duel resulted.
They met in winter, on the snow,
and Pushkin suffered and died slow.

1.XL

At thirty-seven, he proved mortal,
and yet he wrote as if he knew,
his artistry oft like a portal,
and here the wonder of what's true
becomes a musical caesura.
From dotted lines must we infer a
depression greater than portrayed.
As intended, these pages fade
against what I have suffered: ceaseless
desire for sleep—perchance to dream—
a black-hole pull, and, more extreme,
that all should suffer likewise peaceless.
This is the meaning of the lack,
that all suffer this pull, this black:

1.XLI

....

1.XLII

Society's capricious women!
So starts what Pushkin claims is praise
disguised as irony. The whim in
wise Pushkin wants it all both ways.
His ambiguity's pervading,
for Pushkin's truth is found in shading.
You belles, Onegin first ignores.
Our age —says Pushkin— thinks them bores.
Some speak on economics soundly,
but chat with most runs immature.
And they're so smart, devout, and pure,
so punctual (this prized profoundly),
so unapproachable by mien
the sight of them gives birth to *spleen*.

1.XLIII

And you, young beauties, late retiring,
who cross St. Peter's avenues
in daring droshkies (here untiring
Nabokov mansplains what's not news...)
These women lost Eugene's employment.
Apostate of all rough enjoyment,
Onegin locked himself inside,
took up the pen and, yawning, tried
to write—but stubborn work he dreaded,
so nothing new came from his pen.
Nor did he find himself right then
within a guild of the hot-headed,
whom Pushkin really can't condemn,
because he practices with them.

1.XLIV

Again consigned to sitting idle
like half the world in quarantine,
and empty where he should be vital,
Eugene set to—with plans to glean
the thoughts that others represented.

This worthy scheme then regimented
the shelf of books he vainly read.
Some bored, some blathered or misled,
some would all sense or conscience smother.
The older books were obsolete.
The newest groveled at their feet.
As with one courtship or another,
the best-laid schemes gang aft agley.
A pall then hid his books away.

1.XLV
Once having likewise spurned convention
and having vanity eschewed,
our Pushkin showed Eugene attention,
the two fast friends by attitude.
Here Pushkin writes of his affections:
I loved his quirky predilections,
his long obsession with each dream,
his intellect's cold razor's gleam.
I was embittered, he was brooding.
We both had known hot-blooded games,
but life had cooled our heart-felt flames.
Then Pushkin looks ahead, concluding
that sightless Fate and men's dispraise
awaited from their dawning days.

1.XLVI
Who's cogitated—thus existed—
can't but at heart despise mankind.
Whoever's felt, who has persisted,
has borne the ghost of days behind.
For them but nothing still entrances
and them the snake of bygone chances,
that serpent of contrition, bites—
which all does often add delights
and charms to every conversation.
At first, Eugene left me bemused,
but I eventually got used

to his sarcastic disputation,
the jokes laid half with bile and, damn,
the rage in each dark epigram.

1.XLVII
In summer we'd often perceive a
nocturnal firmament so clear,
so radiant above the Neva,
and in the water's cheerful pier,
Diana's face gave no reflection.
Remembering crazy, young affection
and romances that all had been,
now sensitive but chill—again,
we'd get so mutely drunk, elated
on breathing the auspicious night!
Like the imagined forest flight
of drowsy men incarcerated,
our dreams would carry us away
to youthful life just underway.

1.XLVIII
Onegin stood more thoughtful than it
appears in Pushkin's sketch: **regret**
now filled his soul. And here the granite—
not just the Neva's parapet—
recalls both feet and shores: Odessa,
whose polished granite stones express a
connection to that quiet night.
The watchmen called that all was right,
across a distant droshky's clatter.
A lonely boat, with flapping oars,
was gliding far from drowsing shores.
A daring song rose through the patter...
And sweeter still, it would appear,
was romance from this "gondolier."

1.XLIX
O Brenta and the Adriatic!

(This sea's unseen by Pushkin from
Odessa, his aristocratic
exile from Russia's social scrum.
He's building to a moment ruled by
a forefather both seized and schooled by
the czar. Yet African descent
succumbs to poetry's ascent:
the sea is Byron's—Pushkin's quoting.)
I'll love Italian nights of bliss
passed with a young Venetian miss,
now hushed, now chatty, all while boating.
With her my lips will then discove(r)
the tongue of Petrarch and a love(r).

1.L
Is this, at last, my freedom's hour?
It's time! It's time! Oh, I beseech.
I roam the coast, the skies I scour,
I beckon sheets from long the beach.
Beneath storms' vestments, on waves' motion,
along the open roads of ocean,
when will I start to free explore?
It's time to leave the boring shore
of hostile elements who'd shush a
poet, and midst bright southern foam,
beneath my Africa's blue dome,
to languish after gloomy Russia,
where I loved, where it fell apart,
and where I have interred my heart.

1.LI
Back then I had a journey slated
to see some countries with Eugene,
but destiny soon separated
myself from my dear man of spleen.
This was Onegin's father's passing—
and greedy creditors amassing.
Each had a plan for what they sought.

Onegin, happy with his lot,
and truly hating litigation,
left his inheritance to them.
He saw no loss to then condemn—
or had a great prognostication
about his agèd uncle's health:
he would (quite soon!) inherit wealth.

1.LII
Indeed, he then received a letter
from the steward. *Your uncle lies
dying in bed, he won't get better,
a last farewell I would advise.*
And having read the sad epistle,
Eugene departed like a missile:
at once, headlong, and riding post.
Already yawning—bored, almost—
the youth prepared (thoughts of succession)
for sighing, boredom, bedside lies.
(This novel's drop, you recognize.
Yep, fifty stanzas of digression.)
But now a table was his berth,
his uncle tribute for the earth.

1.LIII
Onegin found the manor swarming.
From all around, the dead enlists
a throng of friends and foes, performing
as funeral enthusiasts.
The dear departed they did bury.
The priests and guests chowed down, made merry,
then gravely went their separate ways,
as if they'd wisely spent their days.
Behold Eugene—in country splendor,
with land and water, mill and wood,
this foe of order had made good!
He was till then a lavish spender,
now very glad to say adieu
to former ways... for something new.

1.LIV
Two days Eugene took to discover
secluded fields—a quiet nook—
a leafy grove's cool, twilit cover,
the burbling of a gentle brook
(a common trope Nabokov muddles
with pedantry on lakes to puddles),
but on the third, grove, hill, and lawn
no longer pleased. They made him yawn.
He clearly saw the rural curse is
that boredom's everywhere the same.
Although there was not one card game,
no streets, no courts, no balls, no verses,
depression stayed to stalk his life,
like a shadow or faithful wife.

1.LV
While I, however—Pushkin noted—
am gendered for the peaceful life
and to the rural hush devoted,
where poets' dreams are lively, rife,
and lyres have more reverberation.
Committed to chaste relaxation,
I wander on a lonely strand,
with idleness my sole remand.
Each morning I awake entire
for freedom and the sweetest bliss:
I read a little, sleep don't miss,
and shirk my fleeting fame. Years prior,
I loved the shade. Didn't I laze
right through my most delightful days?

1.LVI
The flowers, love, outdoors, (extinctions),
the fields! To you I pledged my heart.
I'm always glad to note distinctions
between me and my work of art
(and twixt *Eugene* and his translator)

in order that a mocking hater
or publisher of slanderous work,
here ticking off my every quirk,
is not then shamelessly reciting
the portrait's mine (in drafts begun,
though, our two friends would speak as one)—
as if (*as if!*) I can't be writing
a single, sole poetic line
that's not about this life of mine.

1.LVII
I'll mention, by the way, that poets,
are all close friends of fancied love.
I'd dream of a dear thing and know it's
within my soul. The secrets of
these dreams my muse late resurrected,
when I, carefree, praised girls perfected,
the mountain maid, whom I adore,
and prisoners of Salgir's shore
—these women all in Pushkin's writing.
And now, my friends, I hear from you
the all-too-common question: "Who?
For whom is your lyre pining? Plighting?
To whom, amidst the jealous throng,
did you devote its plaintive song?

1.LVIII
Whose glance, exciting inspiration,
rewarded then your thoughtful song
with a caress and fond flirtation?
Who were you praising all along?"
Dear friends, it was nobody! Truly!
I have forlornly felt unruly
desires—the crazy angst of love.
And blessèd is he (writing of
a man, himself, such commonplaces)
who there combines with feverish rhyme:
he doubles the lyric sublime—

following in famed Petrarch's paces—
and calms the heart and claims repute,
while I, in love, was daft and mute.

1.LIX
Love passed. The muse's revelation
then cleared the darkness from my mind.
Now free, I seek the incantation
of sound and sense and thought combined.
I write and feel my heart's not pining.
My dreaming pen is not designing,
nor drawing, near unfinished verse,
those women's feet (his universe).
Extinguished ash has lost its violence.
I mourn, always without a tear.
And soon, too soon the storm will clear
within my soul. All will be silence.
Then I'll begin to write, you know,
some cantos, twenty-five or so.

1.LX
While I was mulling its direction
and then my future hero's name,
I have completed this first section.
I looked it over all the same
and found there countless imperfections.
But I don't want to make corrections.
I'll pay the censorship its due
(and Pushkin would cut stanzas to
appease the censor he had wedded)
and I will give my labor's fruit
to journalists to persecute:
now to the Neva's banks you're headed!
Win me the tribute of acclaim:
misreadings, whirl, words to defame!

CHAPTER TWO

O rus!..
—Hor.
O Русь![*]

2.I
Eugene could get no satisfaction
within that charming country ward.
Though friends of innocent distraction
could thank the heavens, he was bored.
The manor house was quite secluded,
by hills against the winds occluded.
A smallish river flowed below.
Far golden fields and meads would glow
with motley colors when they flowered.
The hamlets twinkled. Here and there
flocks wandered in the open air.
The vast, neglected garden bowered
a refuge where there might alight
a contemplative woodland sprite.

2.II
The august manor was constructed
as manors all should be: supreme
in build and comfort, as conducted
throughout the *ancien régime*.
The bedrooms lofty, you'd discover,
the parlor done in damask cover,
the stoves in multicolored tiles,
and on the walls, the czars' profiles
for whom the censors subbed "his fathers".
All now run down. I don't pretend
to know the reason. Well—my friend
with upkeep hardly ever bothers,
because his yawn likewise befalls
on modernized and crumbling halls.

* O rustic life! —Horace
  O Rus'!

2.III
He settled in the study where for
decades Uncle would criticize
his housekeeper (a marriage, therefore),
stare out the window, and swat flies
(my current U.S. situation—
what's with the flies?) A quick summation:
two wardrobes, table, downy couch,
no speck of ink, for that I vouch.
In the wardrobes, Eugene discovered
a ledger or, if you prefer,
some applejack and fruit liqueur,
and then an almanac that covered
1808: his uncle pled
too much to do, so never read.

2.IV
Alone amongst all his possessions,
Eugene—to pass the time—soon planned
a novel system of concessions.
Hermit sage of the hinterland,
he swapped the yoke of a long-standing
corvée for quitrents undemanding.
The serfs believed him heaven-sent,
whereas one neighbor (thrifty gent)
perceived in this a harm godawful
and to his corner went to mope.
Another smiled—he was no dope—
but in one thing they didn't waffle:
they all agreed, and were quite frank,
Eugene was a most dangerous crank.

2.V
At first all came to pay observance,
but at the neighbors' wagons' sound
along the manor drive, the servants
would bring his prime Don stallion round—
and this, mind you, to the back entry.

Their feeling this affront, the gentry
then ceased all friendliness with him.
"Our neighbor's wild, insane, quite dim,
a mason!" Radical, thus hated.
"He doesn't take a woman's hand,
and drinks red wine, you understand?"
Like Pushkin, he thought vodka dated.
"It's always, 'no.' He'll never say,
'No-sir.'" Such was the shared dismay.

2.VI
A new landowner—that same season—
dismounted at his own estate,
and so the neighbors had a reason
to yet again interrogate:
half fitting Pushkin's self-description,
Vladimir Lensky (in transcription)
possessed the soul of Göttingen,
was handsome, young, a Kantian
—and bard. (The likeness is emphatic!)
From hazy Germany he brought
the fruits of learning: liberal thought,
a spirit baffling and ecstatic,
and ardent speech, not quite in check—
and (Pushkin's) curls, dark down his neck.

2.VII
First-published of *Onegin*'s verses,
presenting a Romantic's prime,
in these next four our bard immerses
the reader in Romantic rhyme.
Not yet benumbed by dissipation,
his soul was warmed by girls' flirtation.
In love, he was so dear (but dumb).
Hope coddled him. The world's new thrum
and glitter charmed his youthful senses.
Sweet dreams would cheer his heart's young doubt.
And the riddle, "what's life about?"—

that grand allure that youth dispenses—
left Lensky wracking his poor head,
suspecting wonders yet unsaid.

2.VIII
He trusted that he'd find affection—
a kindred soul to wed his own—
and that, languishing in dejection,
she'd ever wait for him alone.
He trusted that his friends would crackle
to save his name and take the shackle
and that their hands would never shake
when sent a slander's mug to break.
Our Pushkin was—I guess—uneasy,
and wrote this verse to set friends straight.
And Lensky trusted picks of fate—
blest friends, undying kin—and these he
believed would some time light our ways
and bathe the world in blissful rays.

2.IX
Compassion, also indignation,
pure love of good, and fame's sweet bane—
all roused his blood to first elation.
And with his lyre he'd roam the main,
the plain of Goethe and of Schiller
—essential, this Romantic filler.
His soul burned with their lyric flame.
And, lucky man, he did not shame
the lofty arts of lofty muses:
with pride he would preserve in rhyme
(his) lofty feelings for all time.
Of virgin dreams, he, too, enthuses,
and of their whimsies, then disarms
with songs of earnest, simple charms.

2.X
He would sing love—he love obeyed—and

his song was clear, just as the swoon
of a quite simple-hearted maiden,
a baby's sleep, or as the moon
in the calm void of heaven's splendor,
that veiled goddess of sighs most tender.
He would sing parting and sing woe
and *something*? Something! and then, oh,
the *misty distance*, and then? Roses!
He would sing of that distant realm,
where long his tears had poured to whelm
the lap of peace. And he'd compose his
life's withered bloom—though still but green—
for Lensky was a young eighteen.

2.XI
The backwoods, where Eugene uniquely
appreciated Lensky's gifts,
was home to country feasts held weekly
by squires he'd give the shortest shrifts.
Young Lensky fled their conversations.
Their noisy talk about relations,
and making hay, and hounds and wine,
for him, of course, could never shine
with feeling or poetic fire,
with intellect or witty darts,
with any of the social arts
—why Pushkin *wrote* while playing squire—
but with their spouses, all the talk
was even more a laughingstock.

2.XII
Rich and handsome, with his own manor
he was (mis)took for single, free.
Such was the simple country manner—
and a truth universally
acknowledged: all wished for their daughter
this foreign-bred—"half-Russian"—squatter.
At once the talk, should he drop in,

would take a detour just to spin
the tedium of being single.
They called him to the samovar,
then summoned Dunya (with guitar),
who'd pour the tea, then sing a jingle,
and squeak a line out from a show.
("Dnieper Mermaid," so you know.)

2.XIII
But Lensky, not possessing, clearly,
the wish to turn a wedded slave,
desired a close acquaintance dearly
with our Eugene. Not stone and wave,
nor prose and verse, not ice and fire
so differ as this bard and squire.
At first, in lacking rough accord
with one another, they were bored
and then were pleased. And then the twosome
would meet on horseback every noon
and were inseparable quite soon.
So (Pushkin's first to warrant), through some
shared season, *doing nothing* ends
with strangers now the best of friends.

2.XIV
But even friendship such as this is
won't pass amongst us —Pushkin's peers.
Since having shattered prejudices
(as the Enlightenment reveres),
we now judge everyone as zeros
and see only ourselves as heroes.
Napoleons, we look to be:
two-legged beasts, mere tools, you see,
and feelings an absurd conception.
More tolerant than most, Eugene
still knew and scorned men as routine.
But (there's no rule without exception)
he did consider some select
and others' feelings could respect.

2.XV
He'd hear out Lensky with a twinkle.
The poet's talk and mind ablaze,
his views, yet shifting with each wrinkle,
and endlessly inspired gaze
were for Eugene all new sensations.
He quashed his chilling observations
(or tried, at least), and then he thought
(atypical Eugene) he ought
not thwart this moment of affection.
This season will too soon be done,
and meanwhile let the youth have fun
believing in the world's perfection.
We must excuse the fevered young
both youthful fire and raving tongue.

2.XVI
(It's Pushkin's birthday! And I flatter
that he'd enjoy what I have done.
Our streets alive with Black Lives Matter,
recall he's Africa's grand son.)
And apropos! Deliberation,
which led each friend to contemplation,
concerned the odd past racial pact
and ancient prejudice, in fact,
and good and evil, fruits of learning,
the final mysteries of the grave,
and fate and life. To each they gave
their judgment, and, opinions burning,
the youth recited northern verse.
Eugene obliged—it could be worse!

2.XVII
But often a long-past obsession
would occupy each hermit's mind.
Since having fled their wild possession,
Onegin talked and sighed, resigned.
For blest is he who knew emotion

but then abandoned that devotion.
More blest is he who didn't know,
who'd cool his love by letting go,
by gossip cool his acrimony,
who'd yawn at times with friends and wife,
untroubled by all jealous strife,
and wouldn't trust his patrimony
to a deceitful, goddamn deuce.
That's all for now on cards' misuse,

2.XVIII
since Pushkin cut a fond depiction
—despite compiling Russian ways—
of gaming's draw, well, its addiction.
He claims he's weary of the baize…
When we've convened beneath the banner
of prudent silence, when the manner
of passion has become quite cool
and its compulsions seem the fool,
we love to have another's story
of lawless passion touch us yet.
Exactly as the wounded vet,
with long-forgotten days of glory,
does gladly lean to hear the cache
of stories from a young mustache.

2.XIX
Hot youth can't hide a thing, however,
and gladly blurts out gladness, grief,
and love and hatred to whomever.
Wounded by love (per his belief),
Eugene observed with grave expression,
while, smitten with his heart's confession,
the poet would just share and share.
He would ingenuously bare
his trusting conscience and devotion.
With ease, Onegin recognized
this youthful love that mesmerized,

this story ample in emotion,
emotions that in Pushkin's view
for us have long been nothing new.

2.XX
Perhaps, but now I feel them stronger
within my breast, so Pushkin starts
untrue... He loved as we no longer,
as only poets' crazy hearts
are still condemned to love: in every
moment and everywhere one reverie,
with one habitual rapt prayer,
with one habitual despair.
And neither an excursion's cooling,
nor learning, nor long years apart,
nor hours devoted to his art,
nor foreign belles, nor merry fooling
had changed the soul in Lensky's frame,
then heated by a virgin flame.

2.XXI
When scarce a boy, though, captivated,
still ignorant of love's distress,
he'd been touchingly fascinated
by Olga's childish games. Oh, yes!
His childhood friend's late introduction.
When sharing games was still seduction
and shady oaks with them beneath,
their kin foresaw for each a wreath.
"No. *Garlands*," glossed my Russian tutor,
"worn when the bride bestows her hand."
Chaste was young Olga, lovely and
in bloom. The grass, though, didn't bruit her.
A lily of the valley, she
was veiled from butterfly and bee.

2.XXII
Upon the poet she awarded

the firstling dreams of young delight,
and stirring thoughts of her accorded
the first moan of his panflute's flight.
Farewell to childhood's golden pleasure!
Our budding poet came to treasure
(as any true romantic would)
still solitude, a cozy wood,
and night, and stars, the moon in heaven,
that icon lamp to which we'd bless
our strolls amidst the eve's darkness,
and tears, our secret torment's leaven...
While now the moon's resplendent gleam
seems but a feeble lantern's beam.

2.XXIII
Forever dutiful and humble,
as merry as the morning's rays,
delightful as a loving tumble,
as artless as my poet's days;
smile, azure eyes, voice, flaxen tresses,
and everything Olga possesses...
Take any novel, and you'll find
her darling portrait. Once inclined,
now Pushkin's had enough. And Olga?
Well, nothing rhymes with Olga quite.
Recalling Ellis Island's blight—
how we re-named those from...the Volga—
I'd like to newly name this miss,
but Pushkin's turning to her sis.

2.XXIV
This elder sister was Tatiana...
And such a name! Since time begun,
no poet's put his blessing on a
Tatiana for his heroine.
And why? The name is lilting, pleasant,
though inextricable at present
(this penned in 1823)

from thoughts of Greek antiquity
or of the scullery! We ought to
confess our lack of taste in names.
For verse, our poet makes no claims.
And whether or not Pushkin sought to
promote the Russian tongue's "Plain Jane,"
Tatianas now pervade Ukraine.

2.XXV
And so Tatiana's my selection.
Not by her sister's rosy bloom,
nor by her beautiful perfection
could Tanya captivate a room.
Untamed and silent, rarely cheerful,
a woodland doe, both shy and fearful,
she was a stranger to her kin
and like a true Cordelia in
the reticence of her affection.
In crowds of kids, though still a girl,
she didn't want to play or twirl.
Voilà Romantic introspection.
And oft on quiet days she'd own
the window seat to sit alone.

2.XXVI
Contemplation, her friend, beguiling
right from the maiden's cradle days,
enriched the idle country whiling
with daydreams. And the needle's ways
did never grace her pampered fingers.
Above the tambour frame she lingers,
but she would not enliven cloth
with silken patterns on her swath.
She shows, instead, a taste for leading:
the child in play instructs her doll
(and so thereby herself withal)
in high society's good breeding
and thus repeats (in tones severe)
the lessons of her mother dear.

2.XXVII
But even in the day, Tatiana
would never *take her dolls in hand.*
What's Pushkin mean? To settle on a
translation, Nabokov, offhand,
says it's an idiom. Okay, then.
So to her doll, she'd never say then
the latest styles or news from town.
At childish pranks, she'd only frown.
Her heart would prefer tales of horror
on winter nights. And when their nurse
fetched Olga's little friends diverse,
their endless games of tag would bore her.
No wonder that she would ignore
their sounds of fun, their laughing roar.

2.XXVIII
She loved to wait for dawn's arise on
the balcony, when all is clear
and just above the pale horizon
the dancing stars slow disappear,
and softly the world's edge enlightens,
and wind, the morning's herald, heightens,
and gradually up comes the day.
In winter, when long nights array
in shadow half our earthly numbers
and longer in the idle peace
by the bemisted moon's increase
the lazy Orient still slumbers,
at her set hour, she lifts her head.
By candlelight she leaves her bed.

2.XXIX
Novels became her young addiction.
Romances had her at hello.
She'd fall in love with all the fiction
of Richardson, J. J. Rousseau,
the femme lit of her generation.

Her father, square by inclination,
meant well and saw in books no harm,
but neither did he see their charm,
considering them but idle fodder.
And so he'd never dwell upon
the secret book that dozed till dawn
beneath the pillow of his daughter.
His wife loved Richardson, as well.

2.XXX
Beginning with Cervantes, poets
have warned of novels' dire effects.
We writers seem to want to show it's
our words that twist young intellects.
Tatiana's mother loved quite dearly
this Richardson she'd not read, clearly.
(Her Moscow coz, Alina, told
—and *told*—his tales till she was sold.)
And while engaged, a girl still, bless her,
to Tanya's dad, she dearly sighed
—and *sighed*—to be another's bride.
An ensign in the guards, sharp dresser,
and gambler was her Grandison,
a hero, note, from Richardson.

2.XXXI
Like him, she always dressed in fashion.
But then, not asking her advice,
they dragged the girl (without compassion)
to church (well, *garland*'s more precise).
In order to dispel her sorrow,
her canny husband, on the morrow,
conveyed his bride to his estate,
where she, God knows, would suffocate.
At first, quite overcome with crying,
she just about divorced her spouse,
and then she started keeping house,

which grew routine and satisfying.
Routine is given from above:
a substitute for joy (or love.)

2.XXXII
Routine relieved her ceaseless sadness.
(As it has done in quarantine:
translation has restrained my madness;
a daily stanza checks my spleen.)
She soon discovered total solace.
Mid work and play she found a flawless
secret: an autocratic plan.
Then all went right. She ruled her man.
On Saturdays, she'd take a soaking,
when angry, beat her maids. She canned
fall mushrooms, managed workers, planned,
shaved forelocks on her serfs —no joking!
"To tag draftees," so says my note—
and never asked her husband's vote.

2.XXXIII
In blood, she'd once write memoranda
in albums of her tender friends.
She'd Frenchify their names, demand a
tight corset's lacing to its ends
(of this, I offer no appraisals),
pronounce her Russian with French nasals,
and speak in singing Moscow drawl.
But soon an end must come to all:
Princess Alina's fond discussion,
her corset, books of touching rhyme,
and albums were forgot in time.
She started using names in Russian,
and last of all, she did unwrap
a cotton housecoat and a cap.

2.XXXIV
But still her husband loved her dearly.

About her plans, he wouldn't think
(in all, he trusted her sincerely),
and in his robe, he'd dine and drink.
His life thus peacefully proceeded.
At times, when evening late succeeded,
a neighbor's wholesome family suite,
informal friends, they all would meet
to sigh, to slander, and to snicker
about whatever. Time flows free.
They'd order Olga, *serve the tea.*
Our Pushkin has forgot the flicker
of Dunya—stanza twelve. They sup.
Then time for bed. The group breaks up.

2.XXXV
They, in their tranquil life, kept going
the customs of the good old days:
the piles of Russian pancakes growing
on Maslenitsa —Fat Tuesday's
thin Russian twin, and censors hinted
these seven lines would not be printed.
Here Pushkin wrote about the Church
and customs I don't think besmirch:
they yawned all during service, fasted.
They loved a fortune-telling song,
shed tears on Whitsun blooms... That's wrong?
They needed kvass, he then contrasted,
like air itself and, when they drank
(dined, rather), served their guests by rank.

2.XXXVI
And so they both were growing older,
and in the end, before the man,
the grave then opened to its holder.
A second garland capped his span.
An hour before his lunch he perished.
In death, he was bemoaned and cherished,
by neighbor, children, faithful wife,

more truly than for some in life.
He was both simple and kindhearted,
and there, where his old dust yet rests,
a stone above his grave attests:
Dmitri Larin, first departed.
A humble sinner, brigadier.
God's servant now reposes here.

2.XXXVII
Vladimir Lensky demonstrated
grief at his neighbor's humble tomb,
and to the ashes dedicated
a heartfelt sigh. (We must assume,
though, quoting here, "alas, poor Yorick,"
doubtless made Pushkin's bard euphoric.)
With melancholy, he too said,
"...a thousand times, a child, I pled
to play with his Ochakov medal.
He bore me grinning in his arms,
intended me for Olga's charms,
but feared he'd never see us settle..."
Then Lensky penned, sincerely grim,
a graveside madrigal to him.

2.XXXVIII
And there, in tears, he wrote another
and praised his patriarchal dust
(and this included Lensky's mother)...
Alas! Upon life's furrowed crust,
through fleeting harvest, generations
first sprout, then ripen, fall—durations
others followed (and follow still!)
by Providence's cryptic will...
So grows our flighty tribe and, teeming,
then presses forebears (fact: gives chase)
into their final resting place.
And if you think you're spared, you're dreaming.
Our grandchildren, in some fine year,
will force us, too, from off this sphere!

2.XXXIX
Get drunk on life, friends, for the present!
This living has no point, it seems,
and binds me little—though it's pleasant.
Although I've closed my eyes to dreams,
distant hopes set my heart aflutter.
I hear my Pushkin sigh and mutter;
then: "I'm engaged now," texts my ex.
You fool, it's not about the sex.
To leave a trace, I'd die contented.
I live, I write not for the praise,
but I, it seems, throughout my days,
wished to extol a life lamented
so that a sound, like a true friend,
would me evoke and stay my end.

2.XL
And it will touch the heart of someone.
This verse won't drown in Lethe's straits,
but my creation may become one
of those safeguarded by the Fates.
An idiot pontificating
I foresee, and—vain hope!—his stating,
to mark my famous silhouette,
"I know Tatiana's letter yet!
I'm writing you—a true confession…"
Accept my thanks, Muse devotee,
whose memory will guarantee
my fleeting works' steady accession,
whose gracious hand will so caress
an agèd poet's crowned success!

    2.XLI
    That hope is one the young believe in,
    yet Pushkin knew—though this I stet:
    but then, perhaps, and this is even
    a hundred times more likely bet,
    in dust and soot, unread, and tattered,

my book, along with others, scattered,
ejected from the dressing room,
will end its shameful days in gloom,
like dated schedules or pressed flowers.
And readers both upstairs and down
have equal rights to trash or crown,
yet lack—both equally—apt powers.
I'll be not first nor last to hear
their judgments—jealous, dumb, severe.

CHAPTER THREE

Elle était fille, elle était amoureuse.
—Malfilâtre.[*]

3.I
"Ah, is the day already ending?"
"Onegin, I should go." "I hate
to keep you, but where are you spending
your evenings?" "At the Larins." "Great!
But, Lensky—Isn't it unpleasant
to waste your time there?" "Not at present."
"I don't get it. I see your night
(and, really, tell me I'm not right):
a simple family, proper Russians,
with eagerness to entertain,
preserves, of course, and endless rain
or flax or cattle yard discussions…"
Like his creator, dear Eugene
must catalog all he has seen.

3.II
"I still don't see what's quite so frightful."
"Well, boredom's pretty frightful, friend."
"But your smart set's not so delightful.
The family hearth's a sweeter spend,
where I…" "Again an eclogue! Truly—
enough—my God—and now you're cruelly
deserting me? Oh, Lensky, stay.
And tell me, is there any way
to show me this idyllic maiden
that fills your thoughts and rhymes and pen,
your tears and such?…Present me, then."
And this first confab Pushkin laid in

* She was a girl, she was in love.

demotic verse. Sublime! "You jest."
"I don't." "I'm glad." "So when?" "Get dressed.

3.III
They'll warmly welcome your addition."
The friends rushed off to be enrolled
in that oft onerous tradition,
the hospitality of old.
Thus Pushkin shows our tangled feeling
for pleasure that is unappealing—
a paradox that stalks the book.
Now ritual refreshments, look:
they serve preserves on tiny dishes,
bring lingonberry water, and…
Here Pushkin snipped six lines that spanned
their stay. In quarantine my wishes
are for these customs to resume,
instead of drinks now "shared" on Zoom.

3.IV
Along the shortest route they're flying
at full speed homeward ("winterward"
in a small misprint, gratifying
pedantic critics, who thus spurred
a touchy Pushkin's glossed rebuttal).
And now let's eavesdrop on the scuttle
between the two: "Is that a yawn,
Onegin?" "Habit." "Oh, come on!
You're bored." "No, but it's dark so early.
Andrushka! Faster! Faster! Go!
These stupid places! Apropos:
that Mrs. Larin's simple, surely,
but a dear. Still, I fear to think
I drank her lingonberry drink.

3.V
So tell me, which one was Tatiana?"
"Why, she was in the window seat,

as sad and silent as Svetlana."

"You really love the younger?" "And?"
"I'd much prefer the other's hand,
if I wrote verse. I feel no swoon in
your Olga's face. It's lifeless, like
that bland *Madonna* from van Dyck:
as ruddy as that stupid moon in
that stupid sky." This insult heard,
their ride then passed without a word.

3.VI
And meanwhile, our Eugene's excursion
out to the Larins' caused a stir
and gave the neighbors some diversion.
Conjectures followed in a blur.
And stealthily they all then started
to talk, joke, judge (and this coldhearted)
and plan for their Tatiana's spouse.
Some even swore the marriage vows
were all but pledged and were prevented
because—quite simply—these young things
were waiting for their stylish rings.

What Lensky's wedded fate involved,
amongst themselves, they'd long resolved.

3.VII
Tatiana listened with annoyance
to all this talk, but secretly,
with unimaginable joyance,
she thought of it—unwillingly.
Her heart then took this thought's impression.
As seeds become the earth's possession
to wake and seek spring heat above,
the time had come: she fell in love.

Long since, her young imagination,
now prone to languish, now to brood,
had hungered for a fateful food.
Long since, the heart's slow desperation
constrained her young and virgin breast.
Her soul awaited... have you guessed?

3.VIII
Till... waiting... her eyes opened, beaming,
and dear Tatiana said, "It's he!"
Now days, nights, torrid lonely dreaming—
all only him. And all that she
perceives renews, without cessation,
the magic force of her fixation.
Yet sounds of tenderness conveyed
and glances from a mindful maid
become too much. Sunk in depression,
she can't attend to any guest
and grumps about their leisured rest
and, with atypical aggression,
curses each unexpected call
and drawn out visits most of all.

3.IX
She reads with such consideration
delightful books of sweet romance.
With what vivacious fascination,
she drinks deceptions that entrance!
The strength of dreams has animated
trite romances, all now outdated:
their *Fifty Shades*, their *Twilight* myth,
their Darcy and Elizabeth
in all those poor continuations.
In lovely lines of which I'm awed,
our Pushkin lists what makes him nod.
But for our dreamer, all creations
assume with joy a single mien
and blend into one man: Eugene.

3.X
Tatiana roams the forest's quiet,
now with a dangerous paperback.
Within, the fruits of her heart's riot:
her secret dreams and passion's wrack.
Alone, she sighs. Appropriating
another's rapture, or their waiting,
she then recites, as in a trance,
a letter from this print romance,
a practice that the Slavs do better.
I fear we've lost this soothing art,
for I—a poet!—know by heart
but little verse, much less a letter!
Do note our hero (Tanya's love)
ain't Grandison (op. cit. above).

3.XI
Time was that ardent authors, tuning
their style up to a pompous key,
would flaunt a hero (to those swooning)
as perfect—more than one could be.
This star was always persecuted
(unjustly, sure) and constituted
of intellect and soul and grace
and—always—an attractive face.
With purest passions as foundation,
he, zealous, always did prepare
to sacrifice himself (with flair),
and with the novel's culmination,
vice always did receive its due,
and good received a garland. (True!)

3.XII
Today, all minds are in a fluster.
Morality just makes us doze,
while vice begins to show its luster—
in novels now its triumph grows.
The stories of the Muse of Britain

disturb the sleep of one he's smitten.
This maiden's idol has become
a contemplative vampire, some
Corsair, or... Pushkin lists fantastic,
Romantic fictions now unknown
—for even Byron few bemoan.
Back then, the lord was playful, plastic,
and dressed up in Romantic woe
a hopeless egotism so.

3.XIII
What's this, friends, and can we forgo it?
Perhaps, I tell you, by Fate's will,
I'll someday cease to be a poet.
A novel fiend will drive my quill,
and having scorned threats from Apollo,
in humble prose I'll deign to wallow.
A novel, then, in bygone style,
will occupy my waning while.
I won't depict there evil's bruisings,
but I'll quite naturally detail
a Russian family's fabled tale,
two lovers' captivating musings,
and hospitality of old.
Yes, a callback to this tale told,

3.XIV
but Pushkin drifts. I'll be debuting,
he writes, a simple speech from pops
or uncle, children's rendezvousing
out by the brook or linden copse,
their jealous torments, separation,
and tears of reconciliation.
Again I'll have them fight, although
—at last—garlands I will bestow...
I will recall those words coquettish,
of languid ache so bittersweet,
that, back when at my lover's feet

—oh, Pushkin revels in his fetish!—
there on my tongue they'd come, arranged,
but now, from them, I am estranged.

3.XV
Tatiana, dear! You make me shiver!
As Pushkin aches for her, I him.
I cry, because you now deliver
your fate into a tyrant's whim.
You'll perish, dear Tatiana, perish!
But first, in the blind hope you cherish,
you're summoning a shady bliss.
You're learning of life's languors, miss.
You're drinking yearning's magic potion.
Your dreams pursue you: everywhere
you can imagine an affair
and happy havens for emotion.
And everywhere before you, dear,
your fatal tempter does appear.

3.XVI
Tatiana, troubled by love's aching,
now to the garden goes to brood,
and suddenly she finds she's shaking
and can't walk further in this mood.
Her eyes cast down, her breast now seizes.
Just at her lips, her breath then freezes.
Her cheeks are covered in a blaze.
Sound fills her ears, her eyes with rays...
And night begins. The moon is rounding
its far patrol of heaven's vault.
The nightingale starts to exalt
in arbor's gloom with songs resounding.
That night, Tatiana cannot rest
and softly to her nurse confessed:

3.XVII
"I can't sleep, Nurse. I'm suffocating.

Open the window. Sit right here
by me." "Tanya, what's aggravating
you?" "I'm so bored. I want to hear
of the old days." "I once was able
to recollect an old-time fable,
more than a few true stories of
most wicked ghosts and damsels' love.
But, Tanya, now it's all so woolly:
what once I knew, I've now forgot.
It's really quite a sorry lot!
My mind's a muddle..." "Tell me fully,
dear Nurse, about that bygone time:
were you in love while in your prime?"

3.XVIII
"Oh, goodness, no! We hadn't given
a thought to love back then, or my
late mother-in-law would've driven
me off God's earth." Out came a sigh.
"So, tell me, Nurse, how were you *married*?"
And in the Russian, *garland*'s buried!
"That, patently, was God's decree.
My Vanya was younger than me,
and I was just thirteen, my dearie.
Two weeks the marriage broker came,
and then my father blessed the claim.
I cried from fear. I was so leery.
With tears they then undid my plait.
With songs they led me to my fate...

3.XIX
...and in a stranger's house, by golly...
But you're not listening at all..."
"Oh, Nurse, dear Nurse, I'm melancholy.
I feel so sick. I want to bawl!..."
"My child, you're ailing. What's the bother?
Have mercy and please save us, Father!
What do you want? Do tell... There, there...

Oh, child, you're burning everywhere.
I'll sprinkle you with holy water..."
"No, it's not what you're thinking of.
It's just... you know... Oh, I'm in love."
"The Lord be with you, dearest daughter!"
And with her withered hand, the nurse
then crossed her miss and breathed a verse.

3.XX
"Oh, I'm in love," she whispered, paling,
to the old woman. "Little dove,
my heartfelt friend, you're sick, you're ailing."
"Leave me alone. I am in love."
The languid moon beamed in attendance
upon Tatiana's pale resplendence
and lit her tears and hair undone.
And facing the young heroine,
with silver head in kerchief's cover,
warm in a quilted jacket, shone,
beneath the moon, the ancient crone
(a rhyme from which she shall recover!)
And everything in silence dozed,
by the inspiring moon reposed.

3.XXI
And so Tatiana's heart would breeze in
and out, while she looked at the moon...
A thought was born into her reason...
"I want to be alone—but soon.
First give me, Nurse, a quill and paper,
and move my desk. I'll snuff the taper.
Goodnight!" And here she was alone.
The evening still, the soft moon shone.
Tatiana leans, the ink slow drying,
and writes. Eugene now fills her mind.
And in her reckless words we find
the blameless maiden's love is sighing.
The letter's ready, folded, too...
Tatiana, dear! It's meant for who?

3.XXII
I've known standoffish, distant beauties,
both pure as ice and winter-cold.
Implacable, they knew their duties,
inscrutable to me, all told.
I gawked at stylish condescension
and virtue past my comprehension,
and, I confess, I've run from them
and on their brows conceived this gem
(with modest Pushkin's bawdy citing
all but the "...Ye who enter here!")
Inspiring love for them is drear,
intimidation's more exciting.
You've likely, long the Neva's pitch,
seen such a...word. Well, you know which.

3.XXIII
Amidst obsequious adherents,
other odd women crossed my gaze:
insouciant, with proud forbearance
to ardent sighs and daily praise.
And I am shocked—*shocked!*—to discover
that having scared a timid lover
with stern commands, they still seduce!
A new compassion scores a truce.
A new *tendresse* in conversation
sometimes appears—and further wins.
And doubtless Pushkin, with his sins
(a hundred beds in one collation),
knew blind credulity's young swain
would chase again his belle in vain.

3.XXIV
So where's Tatiana's sin, I wonder?
Is it her sweet belief in dreams?
Or is a simple soul her blunder—
that she is always what she seems,
obeying feelings of attraction

to love without female distraction?
Is Pushkin's darling damned for *that*—
just being in man's habitat?
Or is it trust or being heaven-
endowed with smarts and will, as well,
imagination to rebel,
and tender heart dialed to eleven?
And verily won't you excuse
this thoughtless love she did not choose?

3.XXV
Coquettes do coldly judge contenders.
Tatiana's love, though, is sincere
and absolutely here surrenders,
entrusting like a child, the dear.
She can't believe in speculating
and driving love's price up with waiting—
to better catch in courtship's debts.
She doesn't say, like those coquettes:
we'll taunt his vanity for starters.
(Such hope!) With bafflement we'll next
torment his heart until it's vexed.
Then we'll revive with jealous ardors,
or else this slave, bored with delight,
will solely think of taking flight.

3.XXVI
Still Pushkin sees a complication:
to save his native country's name,
he'll give Tatiana's note's translation.
(A copy's copy's not the same,
and mine I fear will go quite sadly.)
Tatiana knew her Russian badly.
She didn't read our magazines
and didn't really have the means
to give her Russian full expression,
so wrote in French... What's one to do!
I've said that ladies hitherto

would not use Russian for confession,
and our proud tongue would yet oppose
this habit of such postal prose.

3.XXVII
I know that some may see salvation
in teaching mother tongues. (Ukraine
now schools *Onegin* in translation!)
But Pushkin's shocked that ladies deign
to handle the *Well-Meaning* ("phallus,"
as he oft joked in private malice—
a lecher ran the journal.) Friends,
he pleads, don't you write verse to cleanse
your sins by secretly exalting
the ones to whom you've pledged your heart?
And when they speak, don't they impart
to Russian an air sweetly halting?
And don't they give, with wetted lip,
the foreign tongue a native quip?

3.XXVIII
And God forbid I meet, while waiting
on the steps following a ball,
a capped academician prating
or scholar in a yellow shawl!
Like rosy lips without a twinkle
is Russian speech without a wrinkle.
I love each fault, each lapse, each *d'oh*!
But possibly (this Pushkin's woe)
a generation of new beauties,
obeying journals' pleading fools,
will take to teaching grammar's rules
and penning poems as their duties.
But as for me...What do I care?
Tradition is the troth I swear.

3.XXIX
Offhand, mistook—a word at play is

what trembles still my heart amain
(like "Short's the best position they is,"
from Wolff's great "Bullet in the Brain").
I have no strength for reformation:
as youthful sins or styled translation
of La Fontaine, *très chers*, for me,
will ladies' Gallicisms be.
Enough. It's time to take some action
with Tanya's letter long deferred.
Too bad I've given you my word,
for now I'm ready for retraction.
I know: those tender, tender rhymes
are out of fashion for these times.

3.XXX
"The Bard of Feasts and languid sorrow—"
That's Baratynsky, Pushkin's friend,
from whom he would've liked to borrow.
This other bard could apprehend
an ardent girl's exotic letter
and make it magical—what better?
Of course, our Pushkin called. "Please come...
(Like me, he's feeling overcome
with weighing rhyme against narration.)
...and all my rights to you I pledge..."
Yet past the Finnish skyline's edge,
his heart estranged from admiration,
lone, he roams the forlorn massif,
and there his soul can't hear my grief.

3.XXXI
Tatiana's letter sits before me.
I read with secret woe—again.
This treasured note will never bore me.
But who instilled her warmth of pen
and carelessness with grammar's model?
And who instilled such touching twaddle,
such crazy speaking from the heart,

such perilous but gripping art?
I cannot know, but pose, unsurely,
my weak translation, incomplete,
a shadow of a living sheet,
like opera ditties played demurely—
now picked, now plucked, somehow got through
(by pupils Pushkin planned to woo).

3. Tatiana's Letter to Onegin

I'm writing you—a true confession.
What more is there to say, dear sir?
For now, I know it's your discretion
to punish me with scorn, but were
a drop of pity your possession,
you never would forsake a soul
to such as my unhappy dole.
At first I wouldn't speak—no question.
Believe me that the shame I own
you surely never would have known,
if I'd but heard a half suggestion,
that even once a week or two,
in our village I'd chance on you,
or hear you speak, exchange a greeting
or just a word, and then to cling,
to always think about one thing
both day and night till our next meeting.
They say you are unsocial, though,
—and country life is boring, clearly—
but we... While we will never glow,
your presence pleases us sincerely.

So why did you come visit us?
Within our backwoods isolation
I never would have known you thus,
nor known this bitter desperation.
Who knows? In time my maturation
might have subdued my callow mind.

I might have found a kindred person
and been a faithful wife—no worse in
my motherhood, both true and kind.

    Another!...No, I'd not surrender
my heart—no one on Earth would do!
A higher court did judgment render...
God wills that I belong to you.
My life's been all a pledge for later—
for the one date with you I crave.
I know you're sent by the Creator,
you're my defender till the grave...
You'd come to me while I was dreaming.
Unseen, you were my darling, true.
Your voice had long resounded through
my soul. Your gaze, so wondrous, gleaming,
lulled me. A dream? It couldn't be!
When you came in, I knew that second,
and all was shook. With blushing neck and
my face aflame, I knew: *It's he!*
Is it not true I heard you? Pleasing,
in silence, would you not console,
when I would help the poor, the freezing,
or would with prayer begin appeasing
the anguish of my troubled soul?
During this very composition,
was it not you, dear apparition,
who flashed in the pellucid dark?
And were you at my bedside kneeling
to whisper with both love and feeling
a hopeful, heartening remark?
Who are you then? Divine defender
or tempting, treacherous pretender?
Resolve my doubts and make me whole.
Perhaps this is the overstated
delusion of a callow soul!
And fully something else is fated...
But so it is! Henceforth my fate

I will entrust to your direction.
I'm spilling tears as I await
and praying to you for protection...
Imagine this: alone here, I
am understood by not one person,
my force of mind does daily worsen,
and, silently, I ought to die.
I'm waiting now to hear your measure:
revive my hopes with but one glance
or break—for good—this painful trance
with your, alas, deserved displeasure!

     I'm done! Re-reading frightens me...
I'm frozen with my shame and terror...
Your honor is my guarantee:
I trust myself to you, its bearer...

3.XXXII
By turns, Tatiana's groaning, sighing.
The letter trembles in her hand,
and the pink sealing wafer's drying
still on her fevered tongue. Freehand,
in sketches, Pushkin could behold her:
head bent, and from her charming shoulder
her light chemise has fallen so...
Already, though, the moonbeams' glow
is fading. Soon the misty valley
begins to show. The stream adorns
with silver rills, and shepherds' horns
wake villagers with night's finale.
It's morning. Day has now returned,
and my Tatiana's unconcerned.

3.XXXIII
She doesn't see the sun is rising
(a line that should be clear finesse,
but which, I fear, I'm compromising).
With lowered head, she doesn't press

her sculpted seal into the letter.
But gray Philipievna set her
the morning's tea upon a tray.
"Get up, my child. It's time. It's day...
But you, my belle, are up already!
Aren't you a little early bird!
Last night I was afraid. My word,
but now you are quite hale and steady!
And last night's sadness left no trace,
so like a poppy is your face."

3.XXXIV
"I need a favor—with permission."
"I would be glad, dear. Let me know."
"Don't think... please, Nurse... if there's... suspicion...
But now you see... You can't say no."
"My friend, I swear by God—completely."
"So send your grandson—but discreetly—
to take this note to O... yes, that...
our neighbor... with this caveat:
that he not make the least allusion—
and certainly not speak my name..."
"To *who*, my sweet? Oh, I proclaim
that nowadays I'm all confusion.
There are so many neighbors here,
I couldn't count them in a year."

3.XXXV
"How foolish you are, Nurse!" "My dearest,
you know I am already old,
so old. My mind is not the clearest.
It used to be quite sharp, all told.
It used to be a word from Master..."
"What does that matter?" Tanya asked her.
"What need do I have for your mind?
The letter, Nurse, I will remind...
and to Onegin." "Yes, the letter.
My darling, don't be mad. You full

know I'm incomprehensible...
You're pale again—though you were better!"
"It's nothing, really. I'm not worse.
Now send your grandson. Send him, Nurse."

3.XXXVI
But the day passed without an answer.
The next day came, and time dilates.
With ghostly pallor, dressed on chance her
reply would come, Tatiana waits.
For nought. Instead came Olga's dearie,
for whom their mother had this query:
"Where is your friend? I hate to fuss,
but seems he has forgotten us."
Tatiana blushed in trepidation,
and Lensky answered straightaway.
"He promised he'd be here today.
It seems the mail's the complication."
Tatiana dropped her teary gaze,
as if she'd heard severe dispraise.

3.XXXVII
The table glowed as dusk would settle.
The evening samovar, agleam,
now hissed and warmed the Chinese kettle.
Beneath it curled the slightest steam.
By Olga's hand, the tea got going.
The fragrant liquid soon was flowing
across the cups in a dark stream,
and a young lackey served the cream.
And by the window, Tanya'd linger,
then breathing on the freezing pane.
Becoming thoughtful with the strain,
she scribbled with her charming finger,
within the pane bemisted so,
the dear initials E and O.

3.XXXVIII
And all the while her soul was aching.
Her languid glance was full of tears.
Then: clattering!...She started shaking.
Now closer! Galloping...She hears...
Eugene! "Ah!" Like a shadow slipping,
up to another door she's skipping,
from porch to courtyard. And now straight
she flies, flies through the garden gate,
and races, flashing past the edges
of flowerbeds, a bridge and cove,
the lake's allée, a mead and grove.
She broke right through the lilac hedges.
Flying by flowers to the brook
and, breathless now, into a nook...

3.XXXIX
...she fell upon a bench. "He's coming!
What did he think! What must he deem!"
Her heart, with anguish always thrumming,
preserves her hope in a dark dream.
Now trembling, she's ablaze with fire.
But won't he come? The servants' choir
concealed all hint. In garden plots
the maids were picking berry lots,
and they were singing, all by order
(this order based upon the thought
that Master's berries thus could not
be eaten by a crafty hoarder
while busy lips are made to sing:
so rural wit is made a thing!)

3. Song of the Maidens

Beauties, girls so beautiful,
darlings and confederates,
let's amuse with merriment!
Let's spin round, let's pirouette!

Let's strike up some singing, girls,
cherished singing, cherished songs.
Lure the glancing fellow, dears,
to our choral dance-alongs.
As we lure the fellow in,
as we glimpse him from afar,
scatter, dancing darlings, and
patter him with cherries, do,
cherries and sweet raspberries,
currants red—and tasty, too!
Don't you come a-listening!
Cherished song is not for you!
Don't you come a-spying on
maiden games and secrets, too!

3.XL
They sing sweet, and with no attention
to their song, Tanya couldn't wait.
Impatient for the trembling tension
in her full heart to last abate,
for her red cheeks' cool palliation,
her breast beat yet in trepidation,
and her pale cheeks did not return,
but only brighter did they burn…
as a poor butterfly would shimmer:
batting each iridescent wing
while a cruel schoolboy pinned the thing.
Our Pushkin's second trope was dimmer—
a trembling hare—but showed his wit:
like Tanya, he loathed to commit.

3.XLI
But by and by, Tatiana, sighing,
stood up from her secluded stay.
Out of the nook, where she'd been shying,
she stepped and turned on the allée,
where she ran into—nearly crashing—
Eugene, there standing with eyes flashing,

resembling now a threatening shade.
And as though burned, she stopped, dismayed.
But of this unexpected meeting
—and its results—today, dear friend,
I lack the strength to write the end.
Such lengthy speeches are depleting,
so I should rest and take some air.
And then I'll finish with this pair.

CHAPTER FOUR

> La morale est dans la nature des choses.
> —Necker[*]

4.I
Here Pushkin cut six stanzas, so it
allows us time to ballyhoo
the droll digressions of the poet
and the ambivalence all through.
These easily survive translation
and elevate Pushkin's creation.
The first is style, the second truth…
Enough! I'm anxious as a youth.
Like Tanya, I've sent off a letter,
so check my email, check again,
and dread what I may find therein.
Such is the truth, my lot, my fetter.
Yet a romantic, I believe
in purity of love, so grieve.

4.II
With Mykolaiv's isolation,
I never would have known this femme
nor known this bitter desperation.
So why'd I go and live with them?
I'd joined the Peace Corps with some Russian:
serve where they ask, without discussion!
And then the virus brought me home,
my backwoods, with Nabokov's tome,
the brick that's his *Eugene* translation.
He swears (and swears) it's word-for-word,
bereft the beauty Pushkin purred,
and bullies others to damnation,
for only he is Pushkin's peer,
this bitter friend, my Lensky here.

[*] Morality is in the nature of things.

4.III

But why's Nabokov's book so weighty,
when this translation is so slight?
Eugene he wants to arrogate. He
thus overwhelms with notes and spite:
a thousand pages! I surrender.
So while I strive for Pushkin's splendor,
to make his music with my verse,
each compromise strikes as perverse.
Beneath Nabokov's literalism,
I'm bullied, so I doubt my goal.
I doubt my Russian, this book's soul
with ever grievous skepticism.
I blame Nabokov, yet without
his notes, I'm lonely…and I doubt.

4.IV

I'm striving for *Eugene*'s complexion
of lyric loveliness in rhyme,
while using slack for my reflexion:
my joys, critiques, my storytime.
But if, dear reader, you are leaning
to clear ballet between the meaning
and music of *Onegin*, heed
James Falen's or Sir Johnston's read.
One rhymeless day, I sought this second,
to send a line or two of praise.
Some decades dead, he'd spent his days
in Tokyo, Madrid, and reckoned
diplomacy in Arab strife.
His Russian? From his Georgian wife:

4.V

Natalia Bagration was
related to the prince of *War
and Peace*, the general whose run was
curtailed at Borodino, or,
perhaps, much earlier, while loving

a daughter of Czar Paul, whose shoving—
one day the czar expressed his plans
to honor the upcoming banns—
did wed the prince to quite another.
This Catherine was the favored niece
of the Potemkin whose caprice
founded Kherson—and, yes, one other:
dear Mykolaiv, now Ukraine's,
where my Nadezhda yet remains.

4.VI
She charged that I was narcissistic
and wrought *Onegin* as myself.
I thought my goal was altruistic:
my Pushkin on a U.S. shelf.
Ha. Yes, that "my" tells quite the story—
through Homer, Pope and Logue found glory—
but I'd as well as disappear
into the work, like clear Shakespeare
(too, arrogant by any measure),
and Pushkin's wrong. It's not the work.
The work won't last, except by quirk.
For all we know, we have but pleasure,
and doubting, Pushkin's grievous trope.
(Nadezhda means—in Russian—hope.)

4.VII
The less we love, now Pushkin's stating,
the more in love a woman gets
and the more surely ruin's waiting
to catch her in seductive nets.
This cold debauchery was known as
the Art of Love, which—strange, I own—has
proclaimed a joy in shunning love.
But that's a pastime worthy of
the agèd monkeys of the vaunted
occasion of our forbears' run:
the fame of Lovelace (Richardson,

undaunted rake) at last was daunted,
as were perukes and that icon,
the red high heel, their Louboutin.

4.VIII
And who is not bored with deceiving,
restating one thing different ways,
with all that work to sell believing
what everyone's believed for days,
with hearing yet the same objections,
and smashing with the same corrections
the prejudices never seen
by a young girl of just thirteen!
Who will not tire of supplication,
threats, vows, gossip and fancied fears,
deceits, six-page notes, rings, and tears,
both aunts' and mother's observation
and awkward friendship with the spouse!
Thus Pushkin catalogs the house...

4.IX
...but no. Still likeness won't constrict him,
and Pushkin writes, so thought *Eugene*.
In his first youth, he was the victim
of passions free from quarantine
and of tempestuous delusions.
Then spoiled by life's routine profusions,
now with one thing awhile amused,
now with another disabused,
fed up with lust and fickle besting,
heeding in chaos and control
the timeless murmur of the soul,
suppressing yawns with smiles and jesting:
that's how he wasted eight whole years.
The bloom of life thus disappears.

4.X
To fall in love no more beset him,

but he chased beauties anyways.
Refusals didn't long upset him,
betrayals gave him time to laze.
He sought without intoxication
and dropped without consideration.
He hardly felt their love or spite,
exactly as a jaded wight
arrives to spend his night routinely,
with games of whist: he sits for fun
and rides away when all is done.
At home, he falls asleep serenely
and in the morning doesn't know
his evening plans or where he'll go.

4.XI
But our Onegin, on perusing
Tanya's letter, was touched—near fraught.
The language of the maiden's musing
aroused in him a swarm of thought.
And he recalled her with affection,
her downcast eyes and pale complexion.
By then his soul was sunk, it seems,
into delightful, sinless dreams.
Perhaps the heat of past emotions
here seized him for a moment's beat,
but he had no desire to cheat
the innocence of virgin notions.
And now we'll fly across the green,
to where Tatiana met Eugene.

4.XII
The two were still, it felt, for ages.
Onegin then went up to her
and said, "You wrote me several pages,
you can't deny. I read a pure
and trusting spirit's declaration,
a virgin love's exhilaration.
Your honesty is dear to me.

It roused into intensity
what was a long dormant sensation.
But I don't want to flatter you.
Instead I will repay you through
a likewise artless declaration.
Accept my confession, whereby
I give myself to you to try.

4.XIII
"If I had wanted my life bordered
by the walls of the family house,
if a fulfilling fate had ordered
me to become a father, spouse,
if a domestic scene had beckoned,
if only for just one split second,
then, truly, setting you aside,
I would not seek another bride.
I'll speak without poetic shimmer:
in having found my old ideal,
it's only you who has appeal,
to be my friend when days grow dimmer,
to be the pledge of all that's good.
I would be happy...if I could!

4.XIV
"But I'm not fashioned for affection.
My soul is foreign to all play.
So futile is your pure perfection.
I'm not worthy in any way.
With conscience as my bond, consider:
our matrimony would be bitter.
No matter how I love you now,
with habit, I would cease—and how.
You would begin to weep. Your crying
would never touch my heart aright
but would arouse anger and spite.
Judge, then, what Hymen is supplying,
what strain of roses for our bed
and, maybe, for the days ahead.

4.XV
"In all the world what could be rougher
than a household where the poor wife
is day and night alone to suffer
all the unworthy husband's life,
where the bored husband knows her merit
(yet curses fate—so he can bear it),
is always frowning, ever mute,
a coldly jealous, angry brute!
I am that man. And were you seeking
such with your pure and ardent heart,
when writing me without false art,
when such intelligence was speaking?
And can it be that such awaits,
allotted you by ruthless Fates?

4.XVI
"There's no return to dream or season.
I won't reform my soul, I know...
I love you with the love of reason,
more tender than a brother, though.
Now listen here without resentment:
a maiden often finds contentment
in changing carefree dream for dream,
just as a sapling, in its scheme,
exchanges leaves with each spring's turning.
This clearly is the heavens' will.
And you will love again, but still...
Learn self-control. Be more discerning.
No one will see you like I do,
and innocence will ruin you."

4.XVII
What Pushkin drafted as a letter,
so preached Eugene. Vision a blur,
scarce breathing, cheeks becoming wetter,
Tatiana heard without demur.
He offered her his hand. And sadly

(mechanically they say now, fadly—
in 1825, recall)
Tatiana leaned in silent pall.
Her languid head cast down, they started
for home around the kitchen plot.
Though seen together, no one thought
to scold. Our country freedom's charted
its own contented laws, just as
the self-important Moscow has.

4.XVIII
My reader, surely you've reflected
how our Eugene did kindly treat
poor Tanya. (But have you neglected
his final twist, when from discreet
advice came self-directed plaudits?)
Not for the first time, Pushkin audits,
he showed nobility of soul,
although the malice of the prole
found all his failings to embarrass:
abuse came from his friends and foes
(often one and the same, God knows).
We all have foes. From friends, though, spare us!
Indeed, such are my friends, my friends!
Friends I'll remember till their ends.

4.XIX
What's that? Oh, nothing worth attention.
I'm lulled with black and idle dreams.
I (parenthetically) would mention
there are no loathsome slanderous themes
born in a mansard by a liar,
encouraged by the social "choir,"
nor such a vain absurdity,
nor such a vulgar *jeu d'esprit*
that, lacking spiteful motivation,
a friend would not quote countrywide.
All by mistake! He's on your side!

He loves you so...like a relation!

4.XX

Hm! Noble reader, your relations—
are they well? Maybe I should state
just what I mean by a "relation."
The folks with such a designation
are those who demand our respect,
caresses, love, and still expect,
according to widespread tradition,
for us to call at Christmastime
or post a greeting on our dime
—well, *ruble*—just to get permission
to be quite clear of them all year...
God grant them health (and, sure, good cheer).

4.XXI
But then the love that beauties tender
is surer than from folk or friend:
amidst wild storms, you'll not surrender
your rights to love. All comprehend.
But fickleness is nature's passion,
opinions flow round those of fashion,
the whirlwind is the world's renown...
while the fair sex takes flight like down.
Besides, a husband's way of thinking
should always be assented to
by wives of virtue. If that's true,
your loyal friend (or mistress, winking)
will tend to be oft swept away.
And thus with love does Satan play.

4.XXII
So who to love? And who believe in?

And who alone won't us betray?
Who measures feats and stories, even,
obligingly by our survey?
Who doesn't spread a word about us?
No matter vices, doesn't doubt us?
Who spoils us and will never bore?
(This stanza's "trite," Nabokov swore,
and I now do its weakness justice:
"Sur*vey*"? Gar*bage*. "A word"? I mourn.)
Vain seeker of a unicorn,
my venerable reader, trust us,
do love yourself. Oh, worthy find!
There's nothing, truly, that's more kind.

4.XXIII
What was the outcome of the meeting?
Alas, it's not that hard to guess!
Love's crazy suffering kept beating
the youthful soul that craves distress.
No, with a bleak and cheerless ardor,
my poor Tatiana burns the harder.
And restful sleep her bed foregoes.
Her smile, her virginal repose,
her health, the sweet of life, its flower—
another list, which Pushkin meant
as empty phrases, life now spent.
And dearest Tanya's youth grows dour.
Thus does a tempest's shade of gray
attire the just arising day.

4.XXIV
Alas, Tatiana withers, waning,
now paling, growing feeble, mute!
Her soul benumbed, what's entertaining?
The neighbors shake their heads and bruit
in whispers: time, it's time she married!...
(Ellipses, where our Pushkin buried
the failed direction of his plot,

Enough! I'd rather be delighting
imagination with a scene
of joyous love. An unforeseen
compassion, though, impedes my writing.
Thus I must ask your pardon here:
I too much love my Tanya dear!

4.XXV
From hour to hour more captivated
by Olga's young and pretty looks,
Vladimir fully consecrated
his soul to Olga's tender hooks.
He's with her all the time. Together,
they sit in her dark room. Fair weather,
they would spend strolling arm in arm,
their mornings in the garden's charm.
So what? In love's intoxication,
and tangled in their tender shame,
he only sometimes makes a claim—
with Olga's smile as exhortation—
to fondle so a loosened lock
or kiss the trimming of her frock.

4.XXVI
He reads to Olga on occasion
a moral tale, whose author knows
more nature than... *a rhymed evasion*
(Chateaubriand, our Pushkin chose).
But meanwhile, two...three pages, rather,
of monstrous lies or barren blather
(so dangerous to a maiden's head)
he skips right over, turning red.
Withdrawing far from everybody,
they sit at times for games of chess
and lean onto the board to stress
that now they are both deep in study.
Then Lensky's pawn captures a rook,
but it's his own the love-struck took.

4.XXVII
Thinking of Olga yet engages
on riding home, and there, most keen,
he decorates her album's pages.
Now Lensky draws a country scene,
or ink and wash of paint supply her
a grave or dove upon a lyre
or temple to fair Cypris (who
we know as Aphrodite, too).
Now on the leaves of contemplation,
beneath some signatures diverse,
he leaves behind a tender verse,
a daydream's mute commemoration,
a fleeting thought's long-lasting trace,
which many years did not efface.

4.XXVIII
Of course, you've seen the written bounty,
the album of an uyezd miss
(an uyezd being like a county
within the Russian Empire's vis).
This book her girlfriends inked a little,
from start to end and in the middle.
Here spiting spelling, meter's rules,
its verses are tradition's tools
to show a true friendship. Beginning,
Qu'écrirez-vous sur ces tablettes,
inscribed with *t. à v. Annette*
(this French the same in Pushkin's printing),
the album ends, "who more loves you
can write below my fond adieu."

4.XXIX
There, without fail, you will discover
a torch and flowers and two hearts.
You'll surely read vows of a lover:
"until the grave, love never parts."
Some army "poet" (*ours* is haughty)

sure scribbled ditties that are naughty.
In such an album, my dear friend,
I gladly wrote. I won't pretend,
for in my soul I am auspicious.
The nonsense that I undertook
will warrant an indulgent look,
and then the world, with smiles malicious,
won't earnestly investigate
if I could drolly captivate.

4.XXX
But you, you random volumes taken
out of the devils' library,
you splendid albums that awaken
the trendy rhymesters' agony,
you, consummately decorated
by Tolstoy's blessèd hand (related—
this artist—to the writer) or
by Baratynsky's quill (called for—
with The Letter—a lyric favor),
let godly thunder scorch your sheaves!
For when a brilliant lady leaves
her quarto book, with rage I quaver.
An epigram stirs in my soul,
but madrigals one must cajole!

4.XXXI
The form now Pushkin is highlighting
with rhymes that make this stanza's hook.
Not madrigals is Lensky writing
in youthful Olga's quarto book.
His pen breathes love. He's not delighting
in the sparkle of witty slighting.
Of every word and every look
of her, he writes. More truth than book,
the elegies flow like a river.
As you, Yazykov (Pushkin's friend)
in torrents of the heart have penned,

to God knows whom, and will deliver.
Your elegies will incarnate
the total story of your fate.

4.XXXII
Sh! Silence! Do you hear? A crabby
von Küchelbecker (schoolmate, foe)
bids us toss elegy's now shabby
garland. (This harsh critique—this blow—
appeared while Pushkin was refining
Onegin's start.) "Oh, stop your whining,"
von K. cries to our brotherhood
of rhyme, "your croaking as you would,
lamenting yore. Enough! Now sing us
something different!" You're right. You'll ask
for trumpet, dagger, and the mask.
A dead supply of thoughts you'll bring us
to resurrect. Yes?...A big N.
No way! "Write odes, dear gentlemen...

4.XXXIII
...as they were written, as instated
in mighty years, when writing glowed..."
Pushkin belatedly debated
the elegy against the ode.
"What is the difference?" our bard queries
(and I repeat), before he parries
with other talk that's obsolete:
a cunning lyrist is more meet
than our despondent rhymesters? Never!
"The elegy's a trifling shame,
and pitiful its empty aim.
While the ode's a sublime endeavor..."
I'm silent here, argue I might:
no need to see two ages fight.

4.XXXIV
A worshipper of fame and freedom,

Vladimir might have written odes,
but his dear Olga didn't read 'em.
Have tearful bards read episodes
from their own work to their own lovers?
It's long been said that one discovers
no satisfaction greater. (Though
note Pushkin claims he doesn't know.)
The modest lover's blessed at present
when he is reading his own dream
to love and verse's very theme,
the belle so languorous, so pleasant.
And blest...although, perhaps, she flings
herself on fully different things.

4.XXXV
The fruit of dreams, my verse endeavor
I only read aloud with pride,
to my old nurse, childhood friend—never
to rivals of his jealous bride!—
and following a boring dinner,
I always think I'll feel a winner
with some unwelcome neighbor's thought
about some tragedy I've wrought
(then *Boris Godunov*), or—joking
aside—now bored to death with rhyme
and wandering on the lake some time,
a flock of ducks I'll start provoking.
They heed my song of dulcet lines
and fly from shore to soar the pines.

4.XXXVI
Here Pushkin cut a verse expanding
the ducks to hunters and to sport,
with mine—and Pushkin's—most demanding:
to spot the rhymes that don't distort.
There's misery in rhymed perfection
that changes meaning by inflection

and misery in perfect lines
that marry but imperfect rhymes.
Is this the pain of my frustration,
that I can't translate Pushkin whole?
Or am I hunting for control
down South, my corner of the nation
where fires, hurricanes, and fools
vie with the virus and its rules?

4.XXXVII

But what of Russia, that narration?
What of Onegin? Patience, gent!
I will detail his occupation.
Onegin had a monkish bent.
Society he had forsaken.
In summer, six-ish, he'd awaken
and, lightly dressed, out then he stole
towards the river, near the knoll.
He'd imitate Gulnare's sweet singer,
and (vying with Lord Byron's vaunt)
he'd swim across this Hellespont,
then drink his coffee, while he'd finger
a poor review, and dress... in clothes
like Pushkin's, who then cut the pose.

4.XXXVIII

With all his servants, Pushkin couldn't
appreciate my lonely plight.
Without this quarantine, I wouldn't
have known life as an anchorite.
Society I have forsaken.
At eight in summer, I awaken.
With endless coffee, work takes time
—does "tedious" possess a rhyme?—
and nearing noon, I pause translating
to train awhile with kettlebells
(like Leo Tolstoy's Dardanelles)
before my lunch and—still frustrating—

4.XXXIX
With strolls and restful sleep, some reading,
the babbling brooks and forest bliss,
from time to time dark eyes conceding
a pale girl's fresh and youthful kiss
(Nabokov's giddy with delusion:
a pregnant serf in this allusion!),
a steed with discipline and zeal,
a vivid wine, a fancy meal,
a perfect silence and seclusion:
this is Onegin's sacred life.
And he surrendered without strife
to lovely summers sans conclusion.
In careless languor, he forgot
the city, friends, the boring lot.

4.XL
In truth, our northern Russian summer,
grotesque of southern winters, flits
and then is gone, a well-known bummer
that none of us by choice admits.
Already autumn, skies are sighing.
Already days began their shying,
the shining sun less by degrees.
The secret canopy of trees
becomes denuded with sad rustling.
A fog would fall upon the field.
A flock of honking geese then wheeled
and stretched out to the south. And hustling
the boring season to the fore,
November stood just at the door.

4.XLI
The dawn arises in the gloaming.
The field has stilled the sound of work.

With hungry mate to help his roaming,
the wolf emerges from the murk.
Along the road, a horse sniffs, senses,
then snorts. The traveler's cautious, tenses,
and rushes headlong up the hill.
At break of day, the cowherd's skill
drives bovines from the barn no longer.
At noon, his horns no longer sound
to gather all the cattle round.
A cottage rings with maiden song. Her
wool-spinning friend of winter's night,
the kindling crackles, burning bright.

4.XLII
And here already frosts are cracking
and silvering the fields with rime...
(and Pushkin notes his readers' smacking
in expectation of the rhyme
that comes like roses after...frozes?)
More spiffy than a parquet poses
the river, shining, dressed in ice.
A merry band of boys now slice
the ice with vibrant skates. A portly,
red-footed goose, in thoughts about
a swim, tentatively steps out
upon the ice, then slides, falls shortly.
First snows, in twinkling whorls, now soar,
now fall, like stars upon the shore.

4.XLIII
What's there to do this backwoods season?
Go for a walk? The countryside
torments the eye beyond all reason
with naked sameness far and wide.
Or gallop the harsh steppe? However,
uncertain snowpack will endeavor
to catch your horse's dulling shoe
and pitch the creature onto you.

So tuck up in a lonely shelter
and read. Here's Walter Scott, here's Pradt
(French Russophobic diplomat).
No? Check accounts—then curse, or welter
in drink. Long nights will somehow end.
A lovely winter you'll thus spend.

4.XLIV
Onegin, like a real Childe Harold,
then plunged himself in thoughtful spells
(a winter languor not imperiled
by swimming his—quote—Dardanelles).
For, half-awake, Eugene sits first in
an icy bath. Alone, immersed in
the calculations of the baize,
he, armed with blunted cue, then plays
from morn a two-ball game. Already,
the country evening has begun.
The cue is left, the billiards done.
Before the hearth, the table's ready.
He waits for Lensky. Any sign?
Here comes his troika. Quick! Let's dine!

4.XLV
That blessèd wine, Clicquot or Moët,
is quickly brought from the cuisine
—a frozen bottle for the poet.
It sparkles like the Hippocrene
(a fountain sacred to the muses).
Its play and foam like what one chooses
(a splash of Baratynsky's verse—
to which the censors were averse).
Oft Pushkin gave his final lepton
for wine. Remember, friends? Champagne's
enchanted stream gave birth to brains
(ha, not a bit), but joking crept in,
and poetry on varied themes,
and contretemps, and cheerful dreams!

4.XLVI
But it betrays with noisy bubbles.
Indeed, a sensible Bordeaux
I'd rather than those stomach troubles.
For Aÿ—the champagne—I know
I'm fit no more (although I love her).
That Aÿ is most like a lover.
She's sparkling, volatile, and bright,
both willful and a ditz, all right.
Bordeaux, though, you're a friend to savor.
In both disaster and despair,
you're there, forever, everywhere,
and always up to do a favor
or share our leisure's quiet flow.
Long live our friend! Long live Bordeaux!

4.XLVII
The fire has gone out. And sparely
do ashes coat the golden coal.
The fireplace still breathes warmth—barely,
and steam winds upward in a scroll
just visible. Pipe smoke is flowing
up through the chimney. Still the glowing
wineglasses fizz amidst the crumbs.
Gathering dusk, the evening comes...
(I love a friendly glass of vino
and friendly blather well commixed
in what is called the hour betwixt
the wolf and hound. But why? I see no...
No *what*? Here Pushkin doesn't say.
But "golden" coal? That's clear as day.)

4.XLVIII
Now Pushkin's cherished friendly blather:
"Well, then, how are the neighbors? Fine?
Tatiana? Your fun Olga, rather?"
"Pour me another...to the line...
The family's well. They send their greetings.

Ah, my Olga. In all our meetings,
she grows more lovely. Where to start?
Her shoulders! Bosom! Oh, her heart!...
Some time we'll go. They'd be elated.
Or—judge this for yourself, my friend:
two calls, and you won't condescend
to show your nose again. They've waited...
I'm such a knucklehead, I swear!
Next week you are invited there."

4.XLIX
"Me?" "Yes, both Olga and her mother
invite you to Tanya's name day
on Saturday. You don't have other
plans? You've no cause to stay away."
"But there'll be such a whopping babble,
and all that type of common rabble..."
"Oh, there'll be no one. I'm quite sure!
And who will be there? Family, pure
and simple. Let's. Do me this favor!
Well, then?" "Agreed." "A man of class!"
With these last words, he drained his glass—
a toast to Olga. This he gave her
and warmed to talking of his dove,
his Olenka, for this was love!

4.L
As Pushkin nears the chapter's ending,
the plot accelerates. And now
with Lensky's Happy Day impending
(a fortnight hence), he's glad—and how!
Both untold nights of matrimony
and sweetest love's grand ceremony
awaited Lensky's thrilled amores.
He'd never dreamt of Hymen's chores,
the woes and yawning in succession.
Whereas we foes of marriage mark
domestic life as one long arc

of tiresome scenes, a novel fresh in
banalities... Poor Lensky's love
was born for life as told above.

4.LI
Oh, he was loved...at least he thought so,
and Lensky, dear, was happy. Blest
a hundred times is one who's got so
devout a faith, who has suppressed
cold thought and in love's bliss reposes,
as a drunk traveler, sheltered, dozes,
or, gentler, like a butterfly,
now drinking vernal flowers dry,
but pitiful are those creations
who all foresee, whose heads aren't turned,
for whom words, movements, all are spurned
in their oft flawed interpretations,
whose hearts experience did cool
and now won't let them play the fool!

CHAPTER FIVE

О, не знай сих страшных снов
Ты, моя Светлана!
—Жуковский.[*]

5.I

Despite what Pushkin wrote already
about prompt winters of the north,
this year fall weather held quite steady,
while nature long called winter forth.
Snow fell the third of January.
Tatiana woke, as customary,
early, to at the window see
the panes frosted with filigree,
the whitened yard and beds of flowers,
the roofs and fence, the magpies' glee,
the wintry silver on each tree,
and winter's carpet in those hours
that gently draped the rolling grounds.
Now all is brilliant. White abounds.

5.II

Winter!...A peasant, celebrating,
restores a passage with his sled.
His horse, whom snow is stimulating,
now somehow trots with plodding tread.
A daring covered wagon races,
two fluffy furrows in its traces.
The coachman's driving with panache,
in sheepskin coat and bright red sash.
Oh, look! An urchin's put his doggie
in his toboggan and, of course,
transformed himself into the horse.
With freezing fingers from his jog, he
believes it's droll, though throbbing cold.
From the window: his mother's scold...

* O, may you never know such frightful dreams
  My Svetlana! —Zhukovsky

5.III
Throughout, *Onegin* has attempted
the simple plot and Pushkin's gloss,
and so he doubts you would be tempted
by that last scene of nature's dross.
(He's playing coy. Perhaps he's trolling.
That stanza all are now extolling.)
A different poet's rich tableau
would show the comforts of first snow,
and I am sure he'd charm, evoking
in god-inspired, ardent song,
clandestine sleigh rides—come along!
But Pushkin then denies provoking
a feud with Vyazemsky or—worse—
with Baratynsky's Finnish verse.

5.IV
A Russian in her soul, Tatiana
did love, without quite knowing why,
the Russian winter, with its dawn a
belated brilliance to descry
the rosy snow and sleighs so pleasing,
with sunny frost on middays freezing,
with its cold beauty and the gloam
of epiphanic evenings home.
These evenings were all celebrated
according to old Russian ways.
The serving girls these holidays,
by reading signs and what was fated,
promised their mistresses each year
that soldier husbands would appear.

5.V
Tatiana swore by the old fictions
of common folk, and she perceived
in dreams and in the moon predictions.
In tarot cards she too believed.
Signs, symbols, omens were alarming.

Each object had—the thought is charming—
a secret...and to her confessed,
presentiments that clenched her chest.
When a pretentious tomcat, purring
atop a Russian stove, would clean
his face with wetted paw and preen,
she doubtless knew the sign referring:
soon guests would come. And catching sight
of a young moon with horns so bright...

5.VI
...from the left side, she'd pale and shudder.
And when it happened that she met
a black monk, or a hare aflutter
would cross her path, she'd be beset
by fear and doleful premonitions.
She'd full expect—from superstitions—
misfortune soon. (This Pushkin penned
once the Decembrists met their end.
He'd planned to be in that rebellion,
but on the way, he met a fright.
Continue on, he couldn't quite.
The czar hanged high many a hellion,
and you'll still find, on the road there,
a monument to Pushkin's hare.)

5.VII
Back to Tatiana, who detected
a hidden charm within her fear.
Thus Pushkin casually injected
Onegin's weltanschauung here.
Nature, inclined to contradictions,
has so created our afflictions.
Now Christmas season is en route.
What joy! What fun! And foolish yewt
(thanks, *Vinnie*!) tells its fortunes, ever
trusting the future's vast and bright.
Old age, now graveside, weak of sight,

and having lost so much forever,
divines as well, and all's the same:
hope babbles, lies, and plays its game.

5.VIII
With a most curious expression,
Tatiana peers at heated wax,
whose wondrous pattern's poured confession
reveals to her most wondrous acts.
And from a saucer full of water,
they pull their rings in turns. They caught her
small ring to a long bygone song,
which fixed her fate perhaps all wrong:
"Muzhiks have coin there by the fistful.
They shovel silver with their spades.
To them we sing our accolades!"
But warning loss, the tune is wistful,
while singing of a cat connotes
a maiden's marriage, Pushkin notes.

5.IX
The frosty night is clear. The chorus
of grand celestial bodies swirls
in quiet harmony before us…
And having left the other girls
to go outside, Tatiana glows in
her open nightgown. (Is she frozen?
Scared? Pushkin plies the picayune.)
She aims a mirror at the moon,
and it's the *lonely moon* that trembles...
Hark...crunching snow...a passerby...
To him the maiden's tiptoes fly.
Who's there? Her tender voice resembles
a svirel's song. The answer, known,
foretells one's husband. "Agafon."

5.X
Still Pushkin stays with his collation

of common rites. Her nurse then bade
advice for faithful divination.
Tatiana had a table laid
inside the baths for her forsaken,
but suddenly our maid was shaken…
And I, writes Pushkin, also dread.
Svetlana's gotten in my head.
(Zhukovsky's heroine, returning,
too sets for two…) But to divine
Tatiana's fate would cross the line.
She gets in bed. The love god's churning.
A mirror neath her pillow keeps.
Then all grows still. Tatiana sleeps.

5.XI
I want to translate without sneering,
but Pushkin's drafting Tanya's dream.
She's walking through a snowy clearing,
surrounded by her gloomy theme.
From snowdrifts Pushkin says are snowy,
its ripples coming loud and blowy,
appears before her, boisterous, gray,
a stream unchecked by winter's sway.
Two poles an ice block stuck together—
a trembling, deadly little bridge—
are ranged across, to yonder ridge.
Before the raucous, gulfing nether,
her head a jumble, Tanya stopped.
So starts what Pushkin should have dropped!

5.XII
As with a tiresome separation,
Tatiana groans over the strand.
Across, she sees no indication
of anyone to lend a hand.
Then suddenly the snowdrift quivered.
And who, from under it, delivered?
A bear, so big and looking foul.

Tatiana shrieked, and with a growl,
a paw of sharpest claws extended.
She steeled herself. Her hand still shook
when, leaning, that big paw she took.
With fearful stepping, she transcended
the stream and started on her track.
What's this? The bear is at her back!

5.XIII

Lest we forget, Tatiana's dreaming.
The bear's not real. Nothing's at stake.
(Nabokov claims the themes redeeming.)
With quickened step, she tries to shake
her shaggy lackey and his growling.
Ahead, unmoving pines are scowling
in splendor, branches weighted each
with snow. Across the highest reach
of naked aspens, lindens, birches
are shining beams of lunar light.
There is no path. Each bush, each height
was covered deeply past all searches
by the last blizzard. Pushkin, though,
tells us again that all's in snow.

5.XIV

Now in the woods, the bear pursuing,
Tatiana's to her knees in snow.
We know this. So what's Pushkin doing?
Staccato lines, his grammar show
Tatiana's rush, with branches scratching
now at her cheek. And now they're snatching
her golden earring. Powder snow
now grabs her shoe and won't let go.
She drops her shawl, but get it? Never!
She hears the bear close after her.
To lift her skirts, she must demur.
To show her leg, she wouldn't ever!
She runs—and he is always nigh—
until she has no strength to fly.

5.XV
She's fallen in the snow, and neatly
the bear picks up and carries her.
Insensible, she's now completely
subdued and cannot breathe or stir.
He rushes her across the forest,
up to a cabin of the poorest.
Deep in the woods, it's everywhere
forlorn with snow—except one square.
A little window's shining brightly,
and from the cabin, noises blare.
"My godfather's," declares the bear.
"Here you can warm yourself up slightly!"
Into the entry straight he schleps
and puts Tatiana on the steps.

5.XVI
Now coming to, Tatiana's blinking.
She's in a hall. There is no bear.
The door dulls the shouts, glasses clinking
of some funereal affair.
Perceiving this as quite uncanny,
she quietly peeks through a cranny.
What should she see?...A table wound
with monsters, gathered all around.
A witch with a goat's beard is seated.
One beast a rooster's comb adorns,
another, canine snout and horns.
A skeleton is prim, conceited...
Dreams written by a bureaucrat!
Did Pushkin *feel* his crane/half-cat?

5.XVII
All's quite absurd, but not like dreaming,
and Pushkin's monsters yet confound.
Perhaps you'll find something redeeming:
Still curiouser, more profound,
there is a crab astride a spider,

a goose-necked skull in a red miter.
A windmill waves its sails and turns
the Russian squat. (The mill returns
anon, which sends Nabokov reeling.)
Claps, whistles, singing, laughter, woof,
both human tongue and horse's hoof!
Who'd Tanya see? Oh, what's she feeling!
The frightful man she does adore,
Onegin sits and eyes the door!

5.XVIII
He gives a sign, and all fuss after.
He drinks. All shout. Each drains their cup.
He smiles, and all break into laughter.
He knits his brow, and all shut up.
It's clear. He is the boss outright, and
no more is Tanya quite so frightened.
Intrigued, she opened up the door
a crack... A sudden wind then tore
right through, extinguishing the fire
of every lamp and every brand.
Confusion struck the impish band.
Onegin stood, eyes flashing dire.
(Perhaps the glance her letter feared.)
And to the door his way was cleared.

5.XIX
She's terrified. She's trying, failing.
Tatiana can't escape this scene.
Now helter-skelter, Tanya's flailing
and wants to scream. She can't. Eugene
then pushed the door. And with the churning
of pandemonium discerning
the maid, a raging cackle rang
out wildly. Eyes of all, each fang,
all horns, and hooves, and dripping stingers,
the tufted tails, and whiskers, fists
(another of our Pushkin's lists),

the bloodied tongues, and bony fingers,
all indicated her by sign,
and all cried out: that's mine! That's mine!

5.XX
That's mine! Eugene intimidated,
and all the gang at once withdrew.
The frosty darkness instigated:
he and the maid would stay, just two.
Onegin quietly entices
Tatiana to implicit vices
(later this truth makes Pushkin blench)
and lays her on a shaky bench.
He rests his head upon her shoulder.
And Olga suddenly is there,
with Lensky, too. And lights then flare.
Onegin's eyes roam wild and smolder.
A fist reproves the unasked guests.
Tatiana, scarcely living, rests.

5.XXI
The fight gets louder, louder. Quickened
Eugene snatches a knife. A cut,
and Lensky's fallen. Shadows thickened.
A cry past bearing's heard... The hut
then lurched... And Tanya woke in terror...
(This part, at least, is not in error.
On waking, fleeting dreams abide
in feelings, mostly. Look inside
Anna Karenina's beginning:
Oblonsky's smiling from his dreams.)
Through frosty glass, morn's crimson beams.
To Tanya, Olga flies, near grinning,
a swallow fleet and flush as Dawn.
"Who did you dream about? Come on!"

5.XXII
But Tanya offers no reaction.

In bed, she's lying with a book
and turning pages in distraction.
Although this book quite lacked the look
of a poet's sweet fabrication,
of insight, truth, or illustration,
not Virgil, Byron, Walter Scott,
nor Seneca, Racine, and not
a magazine of ladies' fashion
had any reader so abuzz.
Instead, Chaldean wisdom 'twas,
for which Tatiana showed no passion,
save Martin Zadeka, it seems,
was an interpreter of dreams.

5.XXIII
A peddler brought this sage creation
to their seclusion long ago
and, with a (Pushkin-struck) translation
(for Tanya read her Russian slow)
of a French romance now forgotten
(*Malvina* by a Sophie Cottin),
a Marmontel (lost, too, apace),
a grammar, fables, and a brace
of epics (Petriads, retelling
of, yes, Czar Peter's life), all told,
for three and one half rubles sold.
Soon Zadeka showed most compelling...
He eases grief by candlelight,
and Tanya sleeps with him each night.

5.XXIV
Tatiana's dream is most distressing.
Not knowing what this nightmare means,
she wants to find what it's professing,
and from the compact index gleans
an alphabetic list: bear, blizzard,
fir, footbridge, forest, gloom, and wizard
(well, witch) etc. (I smirk

that Pushkin *twice* redid this work.
First: hedgehog? Yes, I cut it. Second:
his "alphabetic list" is not.)
So Zadeka left doubts—a lot—
but dire dreams, Tatiana reckoned,
meant many doleful trials ahead.
For days she'd fret, on some she'd dread.

5.XXV
For several lines our Pushkin quoted
clichés of rosy-fingered Dawn
from Lomonosov, who devoted
his life to knowledge, then took on
a Petriad beyond his measure…
So Dawn brings forth the name-day pleasure.
The Larins' house became the aim.
Whole families of their neighbors came
in their kibitkas (wagons), sledges,
their britzkas (carriages), and sleighs.
In every room a jostling craze:
hellos and bows, guests to the edges,
noise, laughter, shuffling, smooches, chats,
and nurses' shouts and crying brats.

5.XXVI
Accompanied by his plump missus,
the tubby Trifle thus arrived.
Rich master of poor peasants, this is
a Mr. Nails. The Swines contrived
to bear their children in all stages,
from two to thirty are their ages.
In his peaked cap and tufts of down
(from sleeping off his cups in town),
my cousin, Rowdy, you've met, clearly
(from Pushkin's uncle's bagatelle).
Here's Rooster. He's a local swell.
And pensioned councilor Flan is merely
a gossip now, and hefty bloke,
old glutton, rogue, and venal joke.

5.XXVII

The Windpipe family brought the witty
Monsieur Triquet, fresh from the city
(Tambov), in specs and ginger wig.
A true Frenchman, Triquet did rig
a couplet for Tatiana, scoring
Réveillez vous, belle endormie
out of an old anthology.
This children's song he was restoring
by boldly swapping *belle Nina*
out for his *belle Tatee-anah*.

5.XXVIII

Now from a neighboring deployment,
the star of the young ladies' sphere,
the uyezd mothers' great enjoyment,
the company commander's here.
He's come... What news! Superb additions!
We'll have the regiment's musicians!
The colonel's seeing to it all.
What happiness! We'll have a ball!
Already younger maidens gambol,
but dinner's served. In pairs, they go
to dine, now arm in arm, just so.
Around Tatiana misses scramble.
The crowd's abuzz. Men opposite,
all cross themselves before they sit.

5.XXIX

A moment quieted the chatter.
The mouths are chewing. All around
the silverware and plates now clatter,
and glasses clinkingly resound.
But quickly guests rise in emotion

and spread a general commotion.
No one is listening. People scream
and laugh and fight (like Tanya's dream).
With doors thrown open, who should enter?
Our Lensky with Onegin. Awed,
the hostess cries, "At last! My God!"
The guests squeeze tight and from the center
remove their silver. Then they send
for chairs, call out, and seat each friend.

5.XXX
With seats facing Tatiana given,
she's paler than the morning moon,
more trembling than a doe that's driven,
(the early drafts would have her swoon).
Her darkening eyes she never raises.
Within, an ardor fiercely blazes,
and short of breath, she doesn't hear
the friends' hellos. A ready tear
prepares to fall. The poor creation
is near to fainting, but her will
and force of mind were stronger still
(for drama comes in confrontation).
Two words she whispered to the air—
and managed to maintain her chair.

5.XXXI
Dramatic displays of despairing,
and maidens' tears, each fainting bout
had long since passed Onegin's bearing.
Enough of them he'd ridden out.
The crank, caught in this ceremony,
already felt hot acrimony.
Yet noticing a trembling trace
in the languorous maiden's face,
he dropped his gaze. Annoyed and surly,
he swore, indignant, to incite
his friend and get his vengeance quite.

Thus he, now celebrating early,
began what Pushkin has addressed:
caricatures of every guest.

5.XXXII
Of course, Tatiana's agitations
were clear not only to Eugene,
but others fixed their observations
on the rich pie in fatty sheen
(though over-salted, claim my sources).
Between the meat and blancmange courses,
they bring, in bottles sealed with pitch,
Tsimlyansky (sparkling, ruby rich).
Next came the glasses, tall and slender,
just like your waist, Zizi. (A joke—
the real young lady was an oak.)
The crystal of his soul, her splendor
our Pushkin versed in virgin ink:
you phial of love, long would I drink!

5.XXXIII
Once freed of their damp corks, the sortment
of bottles popped. The sparkling wines
hiss, and, with serious comportment,
long worrying his readied lines,
Monsieur Triquet rises. The riot
before him sits, now deep in quiet.
Tatiana's hardly breathing, and
Triquet, the paper in his hand,
turns towards her. His singing started—
quite out of tune. Applause and cries,
and poor Tatiana's forced to rise
and curtsy. The poet, fainthearted—
despite his fame—first lifts a glass
and will, to her, the couplet pass.

5.XXXIV
Congratulation followed greeting.

Tatiana's thanking every guest.
And when the matter reached the meeting
of Tanya and Eugene, her stressed
appearance, languor, and confusion
gave birth in him to an effusion
of pity. Silently he bowed,
but something in his eyes avowed
a lovely tenderness. And whether
Eugene was truly touched or (shame!)
was playing a coquettish game,
by will or mishap altogether,
his glance did tenderness impart,
and this revived our Tanya's heart.

5.XXXV
The chairs are pushed back with a clatter.
The crowd throngs through the drawing room,
as from a tasty hive would scatter
a noisy swarm through fields abloom.
And with a name-day feast that pleases,
neighbor in front of neighbor wheezes.
Seats by the hearth, the ladies took.
Those younger whisper in a nook.
Some open wide the baize resplendence
and call the zealous players to
old ombre, boston, and (what's new)
to whist—all boredom's fun descendants.
(While preferans, of Russian fame,
was my Nadezhda's preferred game.)

5.XXXVI
Eight rubbers have been played by our
heroes of whist. Eight times they've moved.
Tea's brought. I relish that the hour
on all our clocks is here approved
by meals or tea. The country bubble
perceives the time without much trouble:
the stomach is our Breguet.

And I would note—just by the way—
I write as often in my stanzas
of feasts, of dishes, and of corks
(the rhyme our Pushkin over torques
to signify extravaganzas)
as you, good Homer of the spheres,
the idol of three thousand years!

5.XXXVII

The married Pushkin cut two verses
comparing Homer to *Eugene.*
He feared his wife would greet with curses
Istomina, his dancing queen.
And reasons for this fear were ample.
The dancer... Well, here's an example:
she's lured to tea, and she submits
to Griboyedov (*Woe from Wit*'s
famed author). He brings her to quarters
shared by Count Zavadovsky, who
did love the ballerina too.
And "too" because she had supporters,
with Sheremetev paramount,
and, yes, he was another count.

5.XXXVIII

As in a draft of Pushkin's novel,
Count Sheremetev's goaded by
the duelist Yakubovich. "Grovel?
We'll both duel. That's how you reply."
The counts first sought their satisfaction
upon a wintry field. The action
concluded in the bloody snow
with Sheremetev dying slow.
A year elapsed of thought, and writer
met duelist, who did know, they say,
that Griboyedov liked to play
piano, so he shot for spite or
whatever it is called to brand
a pianist right through the hand.

5.XXXVIII 1/2
Staunch Griboyedov long yet lingers
(10 years or so), writes *Woe from Wit*,
and plays piano with three fingers.
A diplomat by czar's remit,
he wanted a U.S. commission.
Instead, he's sent to his perdition.
Upon arrival, he's soon drawn
into mob violence in Tehran.
His body is so mutilated
that traveling to its Georgian vault
he's recognized through dueling's fault
alone by Pushkin, traveling, fated.
(So did he ditch the dancing jewel
to dodge his wife or dodge a duel?)

5.XXXIX
And tea is brought. The well-bred misses
had hardly touched each little plate,
when from the ballroom's doorway blisses
of flute and bassoon resonate.
And by the music's peal diverted,
his cup of tea with rum deserted,
the Paris of the townships near,
this Rooster bows to Olga dear.
And Lensky, Tanya. And our poet
from Tambov takes a Windpipe miss
(an overripe but single sis),
and Rowdy whirled a Trifle. So it
began, this scintillating ball,
and all were streaming to the hall.

5.XL
At the beginning of this fiction
(a look at chapter one's worthwhile)
the Petersburg ball's grand depiction
I wanted in Albani's style.
(Baroque, this painter's now forgotten.)

Drawn off by daydreams misbegotten,
I yielded to the memory
of feet of women known to me.
Oh, little feet, enough forgetting
myself to trail your slender step!
With failing youth, it's time to prep
for wiser words and deeds befitting,
and time, by chapter five, no doubt,
to clean all these digressions out.

5.XLI
Without constraint and yet unchanging,
like crazy youth's unceasing whirl,
the waltz's noisy whirl goes ranging.
With couples flashing, couples twirl.
The minute of revenge beginning,
Onegin, secretly now grinning,
approaches Olga. Quickly he's
out spinning her round attendees,
then seats her on a chair, commences
a tête-à-tête on this or that.
(About two minutes pass in chat.)
The waltz with her he recommences.
Eugene and Olga mesmerize,
and Lensky can't believe his eyes.

5.XLII
Mazurkas past get Pushkin aching:
Time was, mazurkas' thunderous peal
would set a whole great hall to shaking.
Parquet would crack beneath a heel,
and window frames would tremble, tinkle.
It's now not so, that is the wrinkle.
We slide, like ladies, cross the floors
—but in the city. Country mores
preserve mazurkas in their beauty:
the whiskers, heels, the leaped caprice
(like Denisov in *War and Peace*).

There, all remains unchanged by snooty,
despotic fashion, whom we please,
this trendy Russian set's disease.

    5.XLIII
This stanza Pushkin since deleted
about the dance, the spurs, the swing,
and how the women were mistreated
(like horses whipped around the ring).
I long to take Nadezhda dancing,
with singing, drinking, and romancing—
when the pandemic fades somewhat.
I hope, of course, she's waiting, but
if that's not what the Fates have crafted,
I hope she lives without regret.
I want her to be happy, yet
when I read here what Pushkin drafted,
I loathe that I should juxtapose
another's dancing on her toes.

5.XLIV
My brother Rowdy —Pushkin coolly
resumes— up to our hero led
Tatiana and Olga. And, duly,
Eugene, with Olga, went ahead.
He leads her, gliding nonchalantly,
and, leaning, whispers confidantly
some vulgar madrigal to her.
He squeezed her hand, which did confer
to her proud face a brighter fire.
My Lensky saw it all. He's not
himself. (Tatiana's here forgot.)
The poet blazed in jealous ire.
He waits out the mazurka and,
for the cotillion, Olga's hand.

5.XLV
But Olga can't. Can't? That's dismaying.

Well, she already gave Eugene
her word. Good God! Wait! What's she saying?
She could... Could she? Scarce did they wean
this foolish child! A flirt so early!
She knows the tricks of being girlie.
She's been instructed to betray!
And Lensky lacks the strength to stay
the blow. So cursing female ruses,
he leaves to order up his horse,
and off he gallops home. His course:
a brace of pistols he now chooses.
And then two bullets—nothing more—
will quick resolve what fate's in store.

CHAPTER SIX

La sotto i giorni nubilosi e brevi,
Nasce una gente a cui l'morir non dole.
—Petr.*

6.I
Now noticing Vladimir's vanished,
and satisfied with vengeance wrought,
Eugene, with Olga all but banished,
and bored again, sunk into thought.
Behind him, Olga, yawning, glancing
about for Lensky, drooped from dancing.
The overlong cotillion wore
her out, like dreadful dreams. No more.
It's ended. They, to dine, retire.
And beds are made. For one and all,
a place is found, from the great hall
to servants' nooks. All guests require
a peaceful sleep. My Eugene fled,
alone, to sleep in his own bed.

6.II
And all is tranquil. In the parlor,
the heavy Trifle snores nearby
his heavy better half. A snarler
transforms the dining room, where lie
across the chairs Nails, Rooster, Rowdy,
and queasy Flan. Triquet—the crowd he
spurns—is outspread upon the floor,
in jersey, cap, and little more.
The maidens all are seized by dreaming
in Olga and Tatiana's room.
Alone, and sad, pale in her gloom,
her window lit by Diane's beaming,
our poor Tatiana cannot sleep
and looks out on the dark field's sweep.

* Amidst days cloudy and quick,
  are born a people for whom death has no pain. —Petrarch

6.III

His unexpectedly appearing,
the fleeting kindness in his eyes,
his way with Olga—all are filling
the soundings of her soul. She's willing
but can't make sense of him. She stands
a jealous ache, as if cold hands
would squeeze her heart and depths would rumble
and blacken under her... "I'll die,
but death from him is lovely. I
don't grumble. No. Why should I grumble?"
(His name her heart and soul repress.)
"He cannot give me happiness."

6.IV
Now forward, forward with my story!
A brand new face makes his entrée.
Near Lensky's manor—Krasnogory—
about five versts (three miles) away,
now prospering past expectation
in contemplative isolation
(this Pushkin's idyll, sure enough)
lives one Zaretsky, former tough
and hetman of the sharpers' table,
tavern tribune, chief libertine,
but now of simple, kindly mien,
a single dad and friend right stable,
a peaceful neighbor, honest guy:
thus does our era rectify!

6.V
Time was, the public's fawning graces
would praise his wicked pluck. The case:
at five sazhens (a dozen paces),
he'd put a bullet through an ace.
His battles, too, they celebrated:

while thoroughly intoxicated,
he acted bravely in the mud.
Once from his horse of Mongol blood
he spilled and drunkenly did wallow
until some Frenchmen seized this prize.
Each morn, he'd willingly reprise
his bonds... for honor? No! To swallow
three tallied bottles in Véry,
a restaurant found in gay Paree.

6.VI
Time was, for fun he mocked whoever.
Of course, he could deceive a fool—
and famously could fool the clever.
He could be sly or plain (and cruel).
Yet others' tricks would have success in
forever teaching him a lesson.
Yet sometimes, like a dope off guard,
he'd be hoist with his own petard.
He could enjoy himself in wrangling,
retort quite dully or with flair,
at times could hold his tongue with care,
at times could use that care in tangling.
And he could cause young friends to fight
then set their meeting for first light...

6.VII
...or force a reconciliation
so that the three could brunch instead,
and then would spread such defamation
through gleeful jokes. But that time's fled!
Such daring (like that other swindle,
the dream of love) with youth does dwindle.
Zaretsky's refuge from the age
was living like a proper sage
beneath acacias and bird cherries,
two types of tree Nabokov glossed
for fussy pages that exhaust

in telling of the piques *he* carries.
Zaretsky gardens, lives with ease,
and teaches kids their ABCs.

6.VIII
With this Zaretsky, Pushkin shows his
negative capability:
he was no fool, our bard proposes,
and while Onegin utterly
disliked his heart, he did admire
his common sense and judgments' fire.
And since they used to gladly meet,
Eugene was not dismayed to greet
the man one morning. Apropos it,
their dialogue quick broken off,
Zaretsky, with a grinning scoff,
handed a message from the poet.
Then to the window backed Eugene
to read the lines (and all between).

6.IX
It was a gentlemanly, rightly
laconic challenge—or *cartel*:
with cold precision, yet politely,
did Lensky to a duel compel
his friend. From his first inclination,
and turning to this task's legation,
Eugene, without a word undue,
gave *always ready* as his coup.
Zaretsky stood, no explanation.
He didn't want to stay all day—
domestic chores he'd not delay—
so went at once. The isolation
then left Eugene with just his soul
and discontented in his role.

6.X
And serves me right, was the damnation.

He called himself to private court
and charged in strict examination
that, first, he wrongly did disport
to casually provoke the ire
of tender love the evening prior.
And second: let the poet play
the fool. For such naïveté
(he's just eighteen), one makes exceptions.
Eugene adored the youth and ought
to have presented himself not
as a ping-pong of preconceptions,
nor ardent boy, nor scrapper whence,
but as a man of honor, sense.

6.XI
He could have then been open, truthful,
instead of bristling like a boar.
He ought to have disarmed the youthful
heart. "Now it's way too late... What's more,"
he thinks, "the aging duelist's meddling.
He's evil, chatty, rumor-peddling...
Of course, his jests should merit sneers,
but whispers, gossip, nitwits' jeers..."
Again, here Pushkin shows dominion
and quotes his colleague's *Woe from Wit*
(recall the duel, Tehran obit):
And this is popular opinion!
Our honor is the spring that's wound
and sets the world to turning round!

6.XII
At home, the poet now is waiting,
and seethes with restive enmity.
There solemnly the bloviating
Zaretsky brought Onegin's plea.
What tidings for the jealous lover!
He'd feared a flip retort as cover
or some well-fabricated wile

to turn away the pistol's trial.
And Pushkin's plot begins to tighten,
with Tanya's dream and doubts foregone,
and to the mill they've all but gone
tomorrow when the heavens brighten,
and at each other cocked their lead
then aimed at thigh or at the head.

6.XIII
Resolving the coquette is hated,
the seething Lensky didn't want
to see that girl before what's fated.
He watched the sun, the clock—avaunt!
Ambivalence is Pushkin's labor,
and Lensky turned up at his neighbor.
He worried Olenka would shy
and be put out that he came by.
Oh, not at all! As all was prior,
on seeing the unhappy bard,
Olenka leapt into the yard.
Capricious hope, a ball of fire,
she was so happy and carefree,
exactly as she used to be.

6.XIV
"Why did you disappear so early?"
was the first thing that Olga said.
Inside of Lensky, all went swirly,
and silently he hung his head.
And gone were jealousy, resentment
before this look of clear contentment,
before this fond simplicity,
before this playful soul! ...And he
in sweetest tenderness then gazes.
And this he sees: he is loved yet.
And he, so weary of regret,
though ready, cannot find the phrases
to ask his Olga to forgive.
He's trembling, pleased. He wants to live...

6.XV
Is Pushkin's truth the heart's complexion?
Romantic Lensky's love denies
all but his Olga's sweet perfection,
and so *he* needs apologize.
And I, too, want to make concessions.
I want to plead, to write confessions,
because Nadezhda's silence is
my fault, as Lensky knew was his.
I did intend a June returning.
Why'd I not go? The virus, yes,
but it takes two... Nevertheless,
I hope a pilot light keeps burning
to rage into this love I yearn
on my eventual return.

6.XVI
Throughout my life, I've been desirous
of going back to some ideal—
and now to life before the virus.
This seems more true—that's what I feel—
as if I can preserve emotion
from what I left across the ocean.
In these two stanzas Pushkin scratched,
he talks of jealousy unmatched
for misery, that one would favor
the guillotine. But is it worse?
Yes, jealousy remains a curse,
but of the living—a sharp flavor
to bite the soul. While quarantine
is dying slow, alone, unseen.

6.XVII
Vladimir, thoughtful, melancholy,
again before his fiancée,
now doesn't have the strength (or folly)
to jog her mind of yesterday.
He reasons, "I will be her savior

and will not suffer that behavior
of a seducer's wicked blaze
to tempt her heart with sighs and praise,
of an envenomed worm's consuming
the lily of the valley's stem
and thus the flower to condemn
to wilt while still but half-way blooming."
All this to say he does intend,
my readers dear, to duel his friend.

6.XVIII
Had he but known what wound was burning
within my dear Tatiana's heart!
Had she been (wondrously) discerning,
she could have seen life come apart:
how Lensky and Eugene next dawning
would struggle for the grave now yawning.
Her love, perhaps, could all have healed!
But chance had kept this bane concealed,
because Eugene kept ever silent
and our Tatiana pined alone.
Only her nanny could have known.
Had Pushkin let her calm the violent,
this witless "crone" would be the star.
My planned atone? Well, there you are.

6.XIX
All evening Lensky was so scattered,
now silent, now his cheer would rouse.
But then those whom the Muse has flattered
are always thus: with knitted brows,
he'd sit and play lone chords, unhearing,
upon the clavichord then, peering
at Olga with a single thought,
whispered, "I'm happy, am I not?"
But it was time to go. Unspoken
despair squeezed tight his filling heart,
and when, at last, the two did part,

he felt as if it had been broken.
She looks at him. Her eyes implore.
"What's wrong?" "It's nothing." Then the door.

6.XX
Arriving home, he first inspected
the pistols, boxed them up once more,
undressed, then opened and neglected
his Schiller, for one thought is fore.
His melancholy heart is restive:
as Tanya's with Eugene, possessed of
a vision of sweet Olga. Look!
Glorious, she appears. The book
he trades for pen, and verses—crafted
with loving nonsense—sound and flow.
He reads aloud with lyric glow,
like Delvig, Pushkin's friend, who drafted
a verse predicting Pushkin's fame
and, drunk at feasts, would it proclaim.

6.XXI
Yes, chance preserved Vladimir's verses.
Like Tanya's letter, it's right here.
(These Pushkin now calls friends, reverses,
and then becomes their puppeteer—
ambivalence, 'tis his entire.)
"Where did my golden youth retire?
What readies for the coming day?
In vain my glance seeks out the way,
for deep in shadows it lies hiding.
No need. The law of fate is right.
For should the arrow pass in flight
or should I die, all's right, deciding.
Both dreams and vigils reach the mark.
Both blessed are cares and coming dark!

6.XXII
"A ray of dawn will flash tomorrow,

and brilliant day will start to bloom.
And I'll, perhaps, descend with sorrow
into the mystery of the tomb.
Memories of the young bard will follow,
what patient Lethe will enswallow.
I'll be forgotten quite. But should
you come, sweet charm of maidenhood,
to wet with tears the urn forsaken
and think: he loved me, and thereon
he pledged to me alone the dawn
of stormy life untimely taken!...
Warm-hearted friend, beloved friend,
come. I'm your husband till the end!..."

6.XXIII
His writing is *obscure* and *bloated*.
(Romanticism, as it's named,
but I see little, Pushkin noted.
And apropos, Nabokov shamed
the rhyme of *tomb* and *bloom* I granted
the verse above.) Then Lensky canted
his tired head before the dawn.
Where Schiller's word, *ideal*, was drawn,
our poet softly started nodding.
Once he was lost to dreaming's spell,
Zaretsky sneaked into his cell
and woke poor Lensky with this prodding:
"Get up, it's six. And, anyhow,
I bet Onegin's waiting now."

6.XXIV
He was mistaken. At that hour
Eugene was fast asleep as yet.
Night's shadows have now lost their lour,
and Vesper has the rooster met.
Onegin still is sleeping deeply.
The sun's already climbing steeply.
(Yes, Vesper means the evening star,

and the north winter of the czar
brings dawn at *nine.*) Snow glitters, swirling,
but our Eugene is still in bed,
still sleeping the sleep of the dead.
At last he wakes. With curtains furling,
he looks—and sees that it's quite late.
He should have long left his estate.

6.XXV
He quickly rings. In runs his butler,
the French Guillot, who does suggest
his dressing gown and slippers. Subtler,
he hands the linen. Getting dressed,
Eugene tells him get ready, that he'll
come, too—and he should bring the battle
case. Soon the racing sleigh is prepped.
And to the mill Onegin leapt.
He bids his servant take the horses
across the field to the two oaks
and fetch the fateful masterstrokes
made by Lepage. (The man, of course, is
a Paris gunsmith who'd next prime
the czars, thanks to—I bet—this rhyme.)

6.XXVI
Now I recall the sketch of preening
Eugene and Pushkin on the bridge,
for Lensky long awaited, leaning,
impatient, on the damming ridge.
Zaretsky, village tinker, slighted
the millstone till our man alighted.
Eugene comes with apologies.
"Where is"—Zaretsky speaks unease—
"your second?" Classicist in dueling,
he cherished in his heart the *how*.
A pedant, he'd no way allow
exceptions to his strictest ruling,
but followed all the ancient ways
(a thing we ultimately praise).

6.XXVII
"My second?" asked Eugene, composing.
"He's here: my friend, *Monsieur Guillot.*
I don't imagine your opposing
the introduction. You don't know
him, but the fellow is upstanding."
Now Pushkin shows his understanding
of our ambivalence again:
Zaretsky bit his lip. And then
Onegin said to Lensky, "Well—oh—
shall we begin?" "Let's, please." And they
walked past the mill, while far away
Zaretsky, the *upstanding fellow*—
they entered into talks profound.
The foes stand, staring at the ground.

6.XXVIII
Foes! Foes!? Did blood thirst long since carry
the friends apart? Has it been long
since they would share their ordinary
affairs, their thoughts, the dinner gong,
their ease as friends? Today infernal,
like inborn foes whose feud's eternal,
as in a frightening, cryptic dream
(as do Onegin's actions seem),
they coldly ready one another
for death... Should they just laugh instead
of staining their hands bloody red?
(*Here* Pushkin understands the other,
but in his life died from the same—
how social hatred fears false shame.)

6.XXIX
Remark the pistols, gleaming perils.
A hammer clatters at the rod.
The bullets plunge in bevelled barrels,
and triggers click too loud and broad.
Remark the powder's grayish flowing

into the pan. The jaws for throwing
the flint are cocked anew. Behind
a quite convenient stump, you'll find
the shy Guillot. Soon taking places,
the pair of foes take off their cloaks.
And with his most exacting strokes,
Zaretsky counts thirty-two paces.
His friends he parted by this reach
and gave a pistol then to each.

6.XXX
"Now come together." Coldly violent,
but still not aiming, the two foes,
now striding steady, even, silent,
across four lengthy steps did close.
Across four fatal steps encroaching,
Eugene, then ceaseless in approaching,
was first to quietly commence
and raised his pistol in offense.
Now five more paces had been taken,
and Lensky, squinting his left eye,
began to aim as well, whereby
Onegin fired... The forsaken,
appointed hours struck, and so
the poet lets his pistol go

6.XXXI
and lifts a hand, gently concealing
his breast, and falls. His cloudy gaze
evinces death, not pain, not feeling.
Thus shining in the solar rays
upon a hillside, there's a break, and
a clump of slow snow falls. (Awakened)
as momentary chills descend,
Onegin rushes to his friend.
He looks and calls... in vain: the hour
already past, the bard so young
has found an early death unsung!

The storm died out, the pretty flower
has faded in the early dawn,
the fire on the altar drawn!...

6.XXXII
He lay unmoving. Strange was seeing
the languid peace upon his brow.
Below his breast, right through his being,
the wound yet billowed blood somehow.
A tick ago in this narration,
and in this heart beat inspiration,
and hatred, love, and hope would breathe,
and life would play, and blood would seethe.
And now, as in a house vacated,
blank, all in him is quiet, stark.
Forevermore, it's fallen dark.
The shutters closed, the panes negated
with whitewash now the mistress left.
But where? God knows. He lies bereft.

6.XXXIII
It's pleasing to enrage a blundering
foe with a cutting epigram.
It's pleasing to behold his thundering
with butting horns and the "goddamn!"
of shame at glimpsing his reflection
and noticing his own complexion—
more pleasing if he howls, "That's me!"—
but still more pleasing, you'll agree,
is to prepare for him in silence
a just and honest resting place
and calmly aim at his pale face
across a field of honor. Violence
and sending him to forebears, though,
will hardly please you. (Let it go.)

6.XXXIV
Initial drafts showed even leaders

can shameless weep in such a case,
but Pushkin's genius calls his readers,
whom he has put in Eugene's place:
And what if you have felled your brother,
when stares, retorts, or something other
insulted you in liquor's cheek,
or he, himself, in ardent pique
did call you out to pride's acquittal,
do tell me what emotions fill
your heart and soul, when lying still,
death on his brow, he stiffens little
by little at your feet, when he
is deaf to your despairing plea?

6.XXXV

With Pushkin's having primed our feeling,
he can reveal Onegin's course
and we will feel what he's concealing:
with gun in hand, in pained remorse,
Onegin looks at Lensky. "Heck..." and
"looks like... He's dead," Zaretsky reckoned.
He's *dead*!... Felled by this awful thought,
Onegin shuddered, turned, and sought
his men. With care, Zaretsky places
the frozen corpse upon the sleigh
to take the awful trove away.
Now sensing death in twisting traces,
the horses snort. Bits white with foam,
they flew like arrows, straight for home.

6.XXXVI

My friends, the bard has your compassion,
for in the bloom of joyous hopes,
unrealized yet, despite his passion,
unknown, scarce out of swaddling tropes,
he fades! Where is the fierce elation,
where is the noble aspiration
of feelings and of thoughts untold,

all youthful, lofty, tender, bold?
And where is stormy love's desire
and thirst for knowledge and for sweat
and fear of shame and scandal's threat
and you, those cherished dreams entire,
unearthly life's fleet ghost—or *sign?*—
you dreams of poetry divine!

6.XXXVII
Perhaps for the whole world's advantage
or even glory was he born.
His lyre could have had the vantage
to rouse an air across the morn
of centuries. Alas, belated,
perhaps, a lofty step awaited
the poet on our culture's stair.
Perhaps his martyred shade would bear
a sacred secret close forever.
For us has died his vital plume,
and past the boundary of the tomb,
there is no hurry whatsoever
to give his shade a timeless hymn,
the people's way of blessing him.

6.XXXVIII
Perhaps... We nearly see the bitter
philosopher subdue the land:
how Lensky could have fooled with Twitter
and riled with rage the rabble and
the brothers of his age. This story
we've seen of dreadful paths to glory.
But Lensky closed and then was slain,
like the Decembrists whose campaign
was not arrested by a bunny!
While I'm locked in this quarantine
for months and months with my own spleen
to rage against The Man... It's funny,
like Pushkin with this bitter fate,
I'd much prefer to cut my hate.

6.XXXIX
Or, soothes the novel's truth, the poet
perhaps was meant an average dole.
The age of youth would pass, and so it
would cool the ardor of his soul.
In many ways he would have varied:
once parted from his muses, married,
a happy cuckold far from town,
he'd wear a quilted dressing gown.
He'd get to know life intimately,
at forty suffer bouts of gout,
eat, drink, get bored, fat, and worn out,
and, in his bed, he ultimately
would pass away amidst a flock
of kids, sad women, and his doc.

6.XL
But then, whatever he'd discover,
whatever life he may have planned,
the poet, dreamer, youthful lover
was murdered by a friendly hand!
There is a place: near the location
where lived this child of inspiration
two evergreens their roots entwine,
and rills encoil beneath the pine,
runneling from a neighboring hillock.
There reaper women come to cool
their ringing pitchers in the pool,
and there the plowman rests (idyllic).
And by the brook, in the thick shade,
a simple monument is laid.

6.XLI
Beneath this shelter (when spring weather
starts dripping on the fields again)
a shepherd weaves bast shoes together
with songs of Volga fishermen.
A young townswoman, a latecomer

just in the country for the summer,
while crossing fields upon her steed
and bending to his lonely speed,
arrives at this shrine and pulls tightly
upon the reins to check his stride.
Now pushing her hat's veil aside,
she reads with eyes so fleet and sprightly
the simple epitaph. She sighs.
A tear beclouds her gentle eyes.

6.XLII
The open field she's slowly riding,
now having sunk in reverie.
Against her will, her soul's subsiding,
immersed in Lensky's destiny.
"And what was Olga's fate?" she'd wonder.
"Was her poor heart long torn asunder,
or did she quickly disavow
her tears? And where's her sister now?"
(Oh, Pushkin's good! This substitute he's
brought in to guide our thought.) "And where's
the fugitive of talk and stares,
the stylish foe of high style's beauties,
that sullen crank who killed his friend?"
I'll satisfy all in the end,

6.XLIII
but —Pushkin says— not now. Sincerely
do I adore my hero, and
I will resume his story, clearly,
but now I want a brief remand.
The years to solemn prose are sliding.
The years drive naughty rhymes to hiding,
and I—shall with a sigh confess—
limp after them in laziness.
My ancient quill has no desire
to soil with scribbles flying reams.
Now other, cold and lifeless, dreams

and other, stringent, cares conspire
in country peace and social noise
to fret the sleep my soul enjoys.

6.XLIV
I've learned a voice of new desire,
and a new grief I got to know.
As for the first, I can't aspire,
and I regret my former woe.
Oh, dreams! Oh, dreams! Where is your sweetness?
Where's *youth*? (The rhyme makes clichéd neatness
in Pushkin's Russian.) I'm dismayed.
Did my youth's garland finally fade?
Short any elegy whatever,
is my sweet springtime really done
—what I've repeated long in fun?
And is it really gone forever?
And really I'll be thirty soon?
(And I'll be fifty, coming June.)

6.XLV
My noon has come—here Pushkin started
(he'd die at thirty-seven). Fine!
I see, as friends, it's time we parted,
oh, easygoing youth of mine!
I thank you for diverse elation,
for melancholy, provocation,
sweet torments, feasts that can't be missed,
for all your gifts (and every list).
For all, thank you. Amidst the crowded
concerns and in the quiet night,
I took delight in you...and *quite*.
Enough! For with a soul unclouded,
I'm setting off to make fresh tracks,
from my past life I'll now relax.

6.XLVI
A glance farewell to shady cover,

wherein my country days progressed
in languor, passions of a lover,
in a reflective spirit's rest.
But you, oh, youthful inspiration,
enkindle my imagination,
revitalize my drowsy heart,
and to my nook, more often dart.
Don't let a poet's soul stop feeling,
grow bitter, hard, then fossilize
at last amidst the deadening highs,
these ecstasies, this social reeling.
In this whirlwind, along with you,
my dearest friends, I'm swimming, too!

> 6.XLVII
> In first editions, this verse listed
> the whirl Nabokov called a "slough."
> These fourteen lines have yet persisted
> in footnotes; Pushkin kept the two.
> This doubleness of truth, a merit
> in art, becomes, in life, disparate.
> And yesterday we had the jolt,
> our "Januaryist" revolt.
> While I'm aware this will blow over,
> as ill-conceived as what was true
> (our Pushkin's failed Decembrist's coup),
> it roils and threatens like a rover
> the U.S. deck on freedom's deep.
> That battle flag disturbs our sleep.

CHAPTER SEVEN

Москва, России дочь любима,
Где равную тебе сыскать?
—Дмитриев.

Как не любить родной Москвы?
—Баратынский.

Гоненье на Москву! что значит видеть свет!
Где ж лучше?
Где нас нет.
—Грибоедов.

7.I

Released by springtime sunlight beaming,
and finally from the foothills freed,
the snows ran down in turbid streaming
to inundate the sunken mead.
On the year's morn, with sleep retreating,
bright nature smiles serene in greeting.
The heavens shine new indigo.
While yet transparent, forests grow
more green, as if with down and feather.
The bee flies from his waxen cell
to get his tribute from the dell.
The valleys bloom in drying weather.
Herds bellow, and the nightingale
now would the evening hush regale.

7.II

How melancholy is your coming,
spring! Spring, when love begins to bud!

* Moscow, Russia's beloved daughter,
  where can one find your equal? —Dmitriev.

How can one not love their native Moscow? —Baratynsky

–You reproach Moscow, want to travel round?
But where is better, tell me?
–Wherever we cannot be found. —Griboyedov.

What a tenebrous, languid drumming
is in my soul, is in my blood!
With an ambivalence of feeling—
our Pushkin writes—I find appealing
the country calm, its cool embrace
with vernal breezes on my face!
Am I amongst those strange to pleasure?
For all that gladdens, animates,
all that exults and radiates
bores and aggrieves in equal measure
within a soul dead long ago.
Now all appears both dark and low.

7.III
Or do we grieve the new formation
of leaves that perished in the fall?
Does the forests' fresh susurration
recall in us a bitter pall?
Or against nature's resurrection,
do we, in our distressed reflection,
compare the fading of our years,
how each forever disappears?
Perhaps there comes, while contemplating,
amidst poetic reveries,
some other, former, spring, whose breeze
then sets our hearts to palpitating
with dreams of a peculiar night,
a distant land, the moon's pale light...

7.IV
It's time: Oblomov (that good-hearted
"superfluous man," not yet known—
the legacy this novel started)
and every new Onegin clone,
Nestor-gourmands, sires overruling,
you, fledglings of our rural schooling,
you happily indifferent, you,
and sentimental ladies, too,

spring calls you to the country, season
of warmth and works and flowered sights,
inspired strolls, seductive nights.
Quick to the fields, my friends! Now squeeze in
your laden carts, with any horse,
and to the country set your course!

7.V
And you, kind reader (Pushkin flatters),
in your bespoke carriage (calash,
Nabokov says, as if it matters),
give up the city's restless bash,
where you enjoyed yourself this winter.
And with my willful muse, let's hinter!
To hear the leafy thicket's hush
above the nameless river's rush,
where melancholy, lonely, leisured,
Eugene in winter would appear,
in the milieu of Tanya dear,
my youthful dreamer, my most treasured,
but where he no more shows his face...
where he has left a tragic trace.

7.VI
Amongst the hills ranged in a crescent,
let us begin. There a small brook
weaves to the river, effervescent
through verdant mead and linden nook.
The nightingale all night rejoices
in love of spring, and babbling voices
rise from a fount where roses bloom.
A gravestone's seen within the gloom
beneath two ancient pines long sighing,
and its inscription testifies:
"Vladimir Lensky here now lies.
At such an age, for honor dying,
in such a year, was his decease.
May the young poet rest in peace!"

7.VII

Time was, an early breeze convening
would shake the mysterious wreath.
It hung on a pine branch, then leaning,
that unassuming urn beneath.
Two girlfriends once would come. Embracing
in idle evenings, moonlight gracing
above the grave, they'd there lament.
Nabokov claims "I must content
myself with: '...the memorial is
forgot. The wonted trail to it,
weed-choked.'" I guess the phrases fit.
Alone, now gray, a little dull is
the shepherd neath the wreathless limb.
He sings and weaves his poor shoes trim.

      7.VIII

      I understand Nabokov's sharing.
      When meaning, rhyme, and meter fuse,
      I want to give the lines an airing
      and crow the workings of the muse.
      (It is the muse in this translation
      when grace appears in my frustration.
      A cluttered page of broken rhyme
      becomes *right now* a line sublime.)
      I know Nabokov worked his verses,
      but Pushkin's music's a delight
      Nabokov's pride cannot requite.
      He pouts. He preens. He mocks. He curses,
      then burns it down, then is content,
      like our (now former) president.

      7.IX

      This pair of stanzas Pushkin blended
      with those succeeding from his plume.
      They clarify that the intended
      was of the friends at Lensky's tomb.
      And there, above her dear departed,

an uhlan, clicking spurs (uncharted—
these aren't the ones to keep in mind!),
began to charm sweet Olga blind.
Perhaps because these lures elicit
Richard the Third's seductive pull
at a poor husband's funeral,
our Pushkin thought them too illicit
for even Olga's boundless cheer.
Thus history becomes unclear...

7.X
Oh, my poor Lensky! Sad, declining,
she didn't cry for long. The young
betrothed was faithless to repining.
Another her attention swung.
Another offered consolation
with loving praise and adulation.
Now our uhlan could capture her.
And now he got her soul to purr...
And soon with him before the altar,
beneath the *garland*, does she shy,
with lowered head, with fiery eye.
Her slightly smiling lips don't falter.
(Nabokov sees a girl gone wild,
and not the minx who's still a child.)

7.XI
Poor Lensky! Never to awaken,
marooned in deaf eternity,
was the despondent poet shaken
by fateful news of treachery?
Or does he, on the memory-stealing
Lethe, there blessed to have no feeling,
no longer worry disrepute,
for, closed to him, the world's now mute?...
Indeed! Indifference and forgetting
await for us beyond the grave.
The voices of each love, friend, knave

at once go silent. But the setting
of an estate one would exclude:
in angry chorus heirs will feud.

7.XII
But Olya's ringing voice—Oh! Soon it
grew silent in the Larin house.
The uhlan, captive to his unit,
had to return—with his new spouse.
Her tears spilling like bitter water
when bidding goodbye to her daughter,
the dowager seemed scarce alive.
For Tanya, tears did not arrive.
A platitude hid each sad feature
behind a deathly pallor. (Not
ambivalence, but a new thought
our Pushkin had for the poor creature.)
When round the couple's coach all fussed,
she saw them off as we've discussed.

7.XIII
For a long time she remained, staring
as through a fog, and watched them leave...
Now Tanya is alone, despairing!
(Such subtlety can Pushkin weave:
Tatiana's leitmotif is sorrow.
Another grief—I know—she'd borrow.
But whose?...) Alas!—her life-long love,
her confidante, her little dove,
is carried off by fate—forever!
She wanders aimless, like a shade,
the garden's empty promenade...
In nothing is there joy whatever,
and stifled tears relieve no pain.
Tatiana's heart is rent in twain.

7.XIV
And now her ardor burns more proudly

within the brutal loneliness.
And now her heart beats yet more loudly
for far Onegin, no one less.
To see him, though, she is unwilling.
She must detest in him the killing
of her brother... The poet's done,
he's dead. Already everyone
forgets. Already to a second
his fiancée has pledged her sighs.
The poet's memory quick flies,
as smoke across the sky. She reckoned
two hearts, perhaps, were still forlorn
and mourned for him... But what's to mourn?

7.XV
The evening skies grew dark. An eddy
burbled beneath the beetles' buzz.
The dancing folk dispersed already.
A fisherman's campfire was
already smoking, flames appearing
across the river. In a clearing,
by the moon's bright silvery gleams,
Tatiana walked, alone, in dreams.
She walked and walked. A rise did give her
the sudden view of little ville,
a manor house, grove down the hill,
and garden on the shining river.
Tatiana looks—and with a start.
Then faster, harder beats her heart.

7.XVI
She's flustered in her circumspection:
"Shall I turn back, shall I go on?...
He's gone. They don't know our connection...
I'll glance around the house, the lawn."
And down the hill Tatiana's veering.
She hardly breathes. All round she's peering,
bewilderment in her regard...

She enters the deserted yard.
(I here recall Jane Austen's story,
when Lizzie visits Darcy's manse—
hard to believe none looked askance...)
The dogs took Tanya for their quarry.
A brood of boys heard cries amiss,
fought off the hounds, and saved our miss.

7.XVII
"Oh, may I see the house, I wonder?"
Tatiana asked. The childish sprawl
then to Anisya ran for plunder.
(Her keys unlock the entrance hall.)
Anisya came up on the double
and opened wide the house, no trouble.
And Tanya passes through the door
to where *he* lived not long before.
She looks, and in the hall, forgotten,
a pool cue rests upon the baize,
and on a rumpled couch (or chaise?),
a riding crop remains. She's brought in
further and told, "This hearth is where
the master took his lonely chair.

7.XVIII
In winter, he'd dine with his neighbor,
with Lensky, bless his soul. Come, please...
The manor study's where he'd labor,
and take his coffee, be at ease.
Right here he'd hear the steward's warnings,
and read a book to pass his mornings...
(Watch memory now shift its view!)
The former master dwelt here, too.
On Sundays, at his invitation,
I'd come, and at the window bay,
he'd don his specs and deign to play
durak. God grant his soul salvation,
and give his bones a peaceful berth
within the damp of Mother Earth!"

7.XIX
Tatiana, softened in emotion,
looks round the study, at the whole,
and all is priceless to her notion.
All animates her languid soul
with comforts half excruciating:
a desk, and pile of books yet waiting,
and lamp gone out, and rug upon
the bed beneath a window's yawn,
and vista through a moonlit lour,
and this pale light, this falling pall,
and Byron's portrait on the wall,
and, cast in iron, forehead dour
beneath a bicorne, with tucked hand,
Napoleon upon a stand.

7.XX
Tatiana stays. The moment lengthens.
She's charmed within this stylish cell.
But it is late. The cold wind strengthens.
The valley's dark. The grove, as well,
now sleeps above the misted river.
The moon has hidden its last sliver
behind a hill. Now long past gloam,
it's time our pilgrim set for home.
And Tanya, nerves scarce in submission,
and not without a heartfelt sigh,
begins on her return thereby,
but first the maiden asks permission
to visit the lone manor more,
so that these books she may explore.

7.XXI
Tatiana from Anisya parted
outside the gates. And the next day,
the youthful maid early departed
for the abandoned hideaway.
Again within his silent setting,

and briefly all the world forgetting,
Tatiana at long last was left
alone to cry at length, bereft.
Onegin's books then got her started.
At first, she wasn't in the mood,
but the selection he'd accrued
seemed strange. She gave herself—wholehearted—
to reading from Onegin's shelf.
Another world had shown itself.

7.XXII
In drafts, Tatiana read the journal
Onegin wrote while in his youth
about the social dance eternal,
but this was cut. Onegin's truth
is that we know **Eugene vacated**
his love of books—this Pushkin stated—
yet did he spare Lord Byron's art,
and several novels stood apart
for their reflection of the era
and the contemporary man.
Immoral, this ur-superman
was committed to his chimera.
Like some anon, his bitter thoughts
were seething with their futile plots.

7.XXIII
Onegin's pages oft displayed an
incision from a fingernail.
The eyes of the attentive maiden
were quite attracted to this braille.
Tatiana, trembling, sees which notion,
what thought would stir Eugene's emotion,
with what he tacitly agreed
(as I observe Nabokov's read).
The margins show his pencil dashes,
and everywhere Onegin's soul
communicates to her its whole,

unwittingly, now by his hashes,
now by short words that mark his books,
now by interrogating crooks.

7.XXIV
And so begins her understanding.
Thus bit by bit she clarifies—
thank God—the one for whom commanding
fate has condemned her girlish sighs.
A crank of reckless, dour foundation,
was he hell's or heaven's creation,
an angel or a haughty fiend?
(In Tanya, Pushkin's themes convened!)
Is he in fact an imitation,
an unimportant ghost, or yet
a Muscovite in Byron's debt?
A *Childe Harold* interpretation?
Is he a lexicon of trend?...
Is this a parody I've penned?

7.XXV
Has Tanya really solved the mystery?
Now was the answer really found?
(Once Pushkin here did split his history
to watch Onegin go to ground.)
But hours run, and in her labors
she has forgot at home two neighbors
have come to talk her future through.
"She's not a child. What can one do?"
the agèd woman asked, abjectly.
"My Olenka is younger, so
it's time to wed the girl. You know,
to everyone, she says directly:
I won't. What can I do? Her moods!
She roams the woods alone and broods."

7.XXVI
(A neighbor almost solves *this* mystery.)

"Could she not be in love?" "With who?
Rowdy proposed, and now he's history.
And Ivan Rooster—jilted, too.
That hussar, Wheezy (*Wheezy,* is it?)
was charmed by Tanya when he'd visit.
Oh, how the man would bow and scrape!
I thought, perhaps *that* would take shape,
but no. Again, no luck." "Oh, honey,
what happened? Go to Moscow, go.
That's the bazaar for brides, you know!"
"It sounds so nice!... But then, the money."
"One winter is enough, you'll see,
and you could borrow, say, from me."

7.XXVII
The matron quite appreciated
this sensible and good advice.
She squared her books, resolved, then stated
that Moscow's winter would be nice.
And Tanya, hearing news of quitting
home for the city, feared submitting
to judgements of that hard-to-please
society: the qualities
of simple rustic life and (mercies!)
the dated clothes and turns of phrase
attracting the sarcastic gaze
of Moscow dandies and their Circes!...
What horror! No. She'd better stay
inside the country woodland's sway.

7.XXVIII
At dawn's first rays, she wakes and dashes
out to the lays. With softened gaze,
she looks and says (what are rehashes,
perhaps, of innocent clichés
we'd read in Lensky's penned finale),
"Goodbye to you, my peaceful valley,
and you, familiar hilltop climb

and well-known woods. Goodbye, sublime
creation with your blithe resplendence.
I'm trading a nice, hushed domain
for bustle with the brightly vain…
So bye to you, my independence!
Oh, where and why this rushing so?
What will my destiny bestow?"

7.XXIX
Her walks take longer. First a hillock,
now a familiar streamlet stops
Tatiana with delights idyllic.
As with old friends, to meadow, copse,
the youthful maiden rushes, dying
to talk once more, but summer's flying.
The golden autumn has begun.
(How quickly Pushkin's seasons run,
while, quarantined, spring's just arriving.)
Tatiana's nature's trembling, pale,
a sacrifice in fine regale…
And now the North, with storm clouds driving,
drew breath, began to howl, and here
enchantress Winter's drawing near.

7.XXX
She came, and she abounded. Weighting
the limbs of oaks with tufts, she spread
as a vast carpet, undulating
across the fields, around the stead.
The river stilled. From bank to bank, it
vanished beneath a fluffy blanket.
In sparkling frost, we feel so blessed
by Mother Winter's every jest.
Yet Tanya's heart perceives no blessing.
She won't go greet the winter there,
nor will she breathe the frosty air,
nor will she wash, ahead of dressing,
in the first snows from bathhouse eaves.
Her frightful winter trip aggrieves.

7.XXXI

The day of their departure passes,
and then they miss another date.
Inspected, braced, redone with class is
the sleigh once ceded to its fate.
Three sleds—a usual procession—
convey each workaday possession:
their trunks and chairs, big pots for soups,
their feather beds, their cocks in coops,
and canned preserves (oh, so delicious—
my Russian tutor brought me some,
her homemade jams of quince and plum...)
The Larins' packing was ambitious,
and servants' parting sorrows sound,
as eighteen nags are brought around

7.XXXII

to harness to the masters' sleigh (and,
presumably, the other sleds).
The cooks prepare meals for the day, and
the sleds pile high. At loggerheads
are coachmen and the women peasants.
A whiskery postillion's presence
completes a shaggy, wasted jade.
And to the gates raced lackey, maid—
all say goodbye. Amidst the welter,
the venerable sleigh now skates,
now crawls beyond the courtyard gates.
"Bye, quiet spots, secluded shelter!
Will I see you...?" The question dies,
as tears begin from Tanya's eyes.

7.XXXIII

If we remove our Russian nation's
hurdles to the Enlightenment,
the time will come (some calculations
by French philosophers present
a date five centuries hence) when, truly,

highways will change our land unduly.
Roads will connect then intersect,
to form a union more perfect.
We'll step across our widest river
upon a cast-iron bridge. We'll split
mountains, and under seas of brit
bold vaults will engineers deliver.
And, yes, the Christian world will plop
an inn at each and every stop.

7.XXXIV
Now Pushkin quotes another's lyre
in *Eugene's* notes, as if to cite
what all had known: Our roads are dire,
forgotten bridges fall to blight.
At stages, bedbugs, fleas are seizing
each moment's rest. Absent inns, freezing
hovels propose, in restaurant-ese,
sparse "specials," which yet only tease.
Meanwhile, before his flame, Hephaestus
(our Pushkin's "cyclops," village smith)
treats fragile works from Europe with
a Russian hammer. *And who's blessed us?*
he might've bellowed. Ruts are grand,
but potholes grace the Fatherland.

7.XXXV
In winter's cold, this yet reverses:
the driving's easy and quite nice.
As in pop music's thoughtless verses,
our winter roads are smooth (...as ice?)
Our brisk Automedons (Achilles'
charioteer) push lively fillies.
Unflaggingly our troikas drive.
And milestones (versts) so quick arrive,
they flash before the eyes like palings.
Too bad the Larins dragged in fear
of the post horses costing dear

and highways even more. These failings
upon our miss warmly bestowed
a boring week upon the road.

7.XXXVI
(Nabokov spends a page assessing
just when they reached their journey's close.
Two hundred years ago, I'm guessing.
It's *fiction*.) Now before them rose
our white-stoned Moscow's domes. Yet higher,
their golden crosses glowed like fire.
O brothers mine! Oh, what a lark,
when churches, belfries, halls, a park
would suddenly unfold before me!
How often on this homesick sphere—
my fate's to wander—Moscow, dear,
I thought of you, and you'd restore me!
Moscow... The word moves Russian hearts!
So much that simple sound imparts!

7.XXXVII
Behold, on oak-filled territory,
Petrovsky castle, whose domain
takes gloomy pride in recent glory.
Napoleon here hoped in vain.
On recent luck intoxicated,
he judged that Moscow, subjugated,
would bring the Kremlin's keys. But no!
My Moscow would not ever go
to him with head in bent surrender.
No welcome gifts, no holidays.
Instead my dear prepared a blaze
to greet the hero. The pretender,
by thoughts accordingly beset,
then watched the conflagration's threat.

7.XXXVIII
Goodbye, witness to fallen glory,

Petrovsky castle. Well! All right!
Let's go! (Here comes the inventory,
but first...) The border posts grow white.
The sleigh already rushes, dashing
across Tverskaya's potholes, flashing
past balconies, old women, sleds,
lamps, merchants, kitchen gardens, sheds,
stores, Cossacks, monasteries, towers,
boys, fashionable shops, great halls,
Muzhiks, avenues, druggists, stalls,
Bokhars (or Uzbeks), beds of flowers,
past lions playing gatepost boss,
and flocks of jackdaws on each cross.

7.XXXIX

Unlike for most that he deleted,
our Pushkin left no draft for this
omitted verse: no lines completed,
no subpar rhymes did he dismiss.
In Stanley Mitchell's verse translation,
he notes this specious emendation
"conveys a sense of passing time."
Nabokov sees this lack of rhyme
as a furtherance of cheap impressions.
That said, he elsewhere does betray
that Pushkin makes these lists to play,
to see if he could make processions
of authors' names, let's say, in verse—
and in strange tongues, to be perverse.

7.XL

Whatever's meant by the omission,
two hours of this tiring drive
conclude the Larins' expedition.
Around the corner they arrive
from grand St. Chariton's (demolished
when Communists the Church abolished).
Their sleigh before a mansion's gates

stopped. An old aunt (perhaps) awaits,
four years with her consumption pining.
The door's thrown by a gray Kalmuck,
his socks in hand, kaftan amuck.
From the divan, where she's reclining,
the princess greets them with a shriek.
The women hug. Tears wet each cheek.

7.XLI
"*Mon ange!*" "Pachette!" "Alina, dearie!"
"Who would have thought? How long it's been!
Will you stay long? Oh, dear, I'm teary!
But sit...how strange! Where to begin?
Like something from a novel's plot or..."
"This is Tatiana, my dear daughter."
"Ah, Tanya! Come to me. I seem
as if I'm living in a dream...
Now, cousin—Grandison, remember?"
"What Grandison?... Oh! *Grandison*!
Where is he?" "Near Saint Simeon—
in Moscow, love. Just in December
he came by, pleased as anyone.
He'd lately married off a son.

7.XLII
"As for the other one... but later
we'll talk of everything, all right?
And Tanya, oh, we'll inundate her
with relatives tomorrow bright
and early. Pity, I no longer
can go about. I once was stronger,
but now my legs are quite the load.
Oh, you're exhausted from the road.
Let's go and rest... My chest is weary...
Now even joy for me is tough,
not just despair... I'm fit enough,
my dear, for nowhere... It's so dreary...
Old age is horrid..." Breaking off,
now spent, in tears, she starts to cough.

7.XLIII
The gaiety and the caresses
of Tanya's ailing auntie stir
her pity, but the home depresses.
Like Proust, Tatiana's used to her
own room. Behind a silken curtain,
in a new bed, her sleep's uncertain.
The ringing church bells' early sounds,
precursor to the morning rounds,
arouse her from her slumber. Seated
at the window when shadows thin,
Tatiana can't discern within
her own sweet fields. Instead, she's greeted
by a strange yard that makes no sense:
a stranger's stable, cookhouse, fence.

7.XLIV
And rounds of family invitations
drain Tanya through their endless stints
of showing elderly relations
her absentminded indolence.
Now distant kin, without exception,
will always get a fond reception,
with bread and salt (the Slavic rite
that welcomed to my Peace Corps site)
and the same timeless exclamations:
"How much you've grown! How many years
since I held you! Or boxed your ears!
Or fed you cookies!" Old relations
then join in chorus and bemoan,
"Oh, dear! How fast the years have flown!"

7.XLV
Whereas in them, none see the changes,
for everything remains old school.
Sweet Aunt Elena still arranges
her hair within a cap of tulle.
Still pale—Lukeria Livovna.

Still slandering is Lyubov Petrovna.
Her brother Ivan's still a stooge.
Semyon, the other's still a Scrooge.
Aunt Pelageya's still maintaining
her friend Monsieur Finemouche, her spitz,
her husband, who still never quits
his club. The man's still uncomplaining,
still meek and deaf, eats twice his size
(and in the drafts, still swats at flies!)

7.XLVI
Their girls greet Tanya with embraces.
At first, they silently run down,
as Moscow's young and trendy graces,
our Tanya to her foot from crown.
They find her strange (well, unexpected),
a bit provincial and affected,
and somewhat pale, and thin—a tad—
but then again, her looks aren't bad.
In time, submitting to compassion,
the girls make friends, invite her (pleeeeaase),
give kisses—and her hand a squeeze.
They fluff her hair (as was the fashion),
and, in a whispered lilt, impart
the secrets of a girlish heart,

7.XLVII
their own and others' sweet successes,
with hopes and pranks, and dreams held dear.
Thus innocently talk progresses
with varnish of the easy smear.
And then in payment for this chatter,
they do require—while they flatter—
a true confession of the heart.
Our Tanya, though, does not take part.
She hears the talk as if she's sleeping,
and nothing does she grasp thereof.
The secrets of her heart and love,

the cherished store of joys and weeping,
she keeps in silence. On the whole,
she doesn't share—not with a soul.

7.XLVIII
Tatiana wants to listen closely
to the discussion and the talk,
but everyone is taken mostly
by incoherent, vapid schlock.
In everything, they're stale and tired.
Their slander's even uninspired.
Within this fruitless chill of views,
of questions, gossip, and of news,
for days and nights a thought won't flicker—
not by surprise or random word.
A youthful heart won't there be stirred.
A languid mind won't smile, nor snicker.
Dumb joking, even, won't be met
in you, the superficial set.

7.XLIX
Aloofly watching and conversing
distaste of Tanya mongst themselves
are young archivists (nobles nursing
their sinecures midst bureau shelves).
And at the door, a sorry jester
found her "ideal" and so addressed her
an elegy. At a dull aunt's,
dear Vyazemsky, by novel chance,
sat down beside our lovely maiden—
through Pushkin's friendship, apropos:
the chapter five shout-out on snow—
he piqued her soul. An old man weighed in,
after adjusting his toupee,
and asked about our Tanya's day.

7.L
But where the tempest of the roaring

Melpomene resounds so long,
and where she brandishes her soaring,
flamboyant cloak to the cold throng,
where Thalia serenely lazes
and doesn't heed the friendly praises,
where by Terpsichore alone,
young fans see marvels unbeknown
(Istomina was Pushkin's danger),
the ladies' envious lorgnettes
and faddish experts' fickle têtes
did not there turn to spy the stranger,
unlike in drafts, where Pushkin's pet
became the focus of that set.

7.LI
Then to a nobles' club they send her:
Sobrania, where crush, thrill, heat,
the music's clamor, candles' splendor,
the flashing whirl of lively feet,
the beauties in their light regalia,
the galleries' bright bacchanalia,
and maidens gathered in a ring
together make the senses sing.
And zealous dandies, each here flaunted
his impudence, flamboyant vest,
that his lorgnette was unimpressed.
And hussars now on leave here jaunted
to jangle, roar, make their entrée,
to captivate and fly away.

7.LII
The nightly sky has lovely glisters,
and Moscow has its beauties, too,
but brighter than the heaven's sisters
remains the moon in airy blue.
And she, whose name's still in sequester,
is one I would not dare to pester
upon my lyre's poetic swells.

Like the majestic moon, twixt belles
and beauts, she shines alone. She brushes
the earth with proud, celestial dance!
How languid is her lovely glance!
What relish fills her breast! So lush is—
But now, enough, enough. Just cease.
You've paid your foolishness its piece.

7.LIII
Noise, laughter, bustle, bowing, (filler),
quadrille, mazurka, waltz... Here notched
between two aunties, near a pillar,
remarked by no one, Tanya watched
but saw nothing. She hates the stresses
of social whirls. Here all oppresses...
(Oh, *Madame Bovary, c'est moi!*)
Through dreams, our Tanya feels the draw
to country fields, the poor, the bowers.
She's drawn to the secluded nook
where flows the small, pellucid brook,
and to her novels and her flowers,
to dusk beneath the linden tree,
where who appeared to her? Why, *he.*

7.LIV
So Tanya's thoughts quite far meander,
forgetting world and noisy ball,
and some grand general's brash gander
remains forever in her thrall.
The aunties wink in understanding
and elbow Tanya, now demanding,
with urgent whispering to her,
"Look left. Be quick. Don't cause a stir."
"Where? Left? But what's so fascinating?"
"Well, dear, what's there is there. Don't stare!...
That group, you see? Ahead, just there,
where two in uniform are waiting...
Now look... He's stepping into view..."
"That portly general? That's who?"

7.LV
But here we give congratulation
for Tanya's conquest on that night
and take ourselves a divagation,
so not to lose of whom I write...
In Pushkin's planning for this turn, he
wanted to share Onegin's journey
down to Odessa (dear Ukraine!),
where words of quarantines make plain
this book contains the world entire.
But Pushkin cut this in a huff.
Critiques of Tanya's trip were rough—
though critics had yet to conspire.
For now he begs his muse to sing
his youthful friend, his every fling.

CHAPTER EIGHT

Fare thee well, and if for ever
Still for ever fare thee well.
—Byron.

8.I
Those days, in the Lyceum's garden,
I would serenely flourish so.
I read with pleasure in that Arden
The Golden Ass, not Cicero.
In those old days, in secret valleys,
in springtime with the swans' loud sallies,
near pools lit in tranquility,
the muse began to visit me.
My cell within the dormitory
at once grew light, and there my muse
revealed a feast of young taboos.
She praised in song our ancient glory.
Of childish joys she sang esteem.
She hailed the heart's most trembling dream.

8.II
The public smiled at her reception,
and first successes made us brave.
Derzhavin—poet of exception—
bestowed his blessing at the grave.
(Since these four lines give us the essence,
the rest were cut, and adolescence—
six stanzas—trimmed to one above.
Having no early muse, no love,
I idealize this, the appearance
of Pushkin's verse within his set.
As an American, I sweat.
I only have the perseverance
that got a rover late to Mars
and keeps me striving for the stars.)

8.III
But, Pushkin writes, I took the notion
of passion's rule to be my creed.
Longing to share my young emotion,
my frisky muse I'd gladly lead
to noisy feasts and wild debating
(and night patrols she relished baiting).
Within the rowdy banquet hall,
she would present her gifts to all,
and as a slight bacchante, she gamboled
across the cups and through the haze.
She sang, and youths of bygone days
behind my muse then madly scrambled.
Amongst my friends, I would enshrine
this fair capricious girl of mine.

8.IV
But from these friends I separated
(so exile Pushkin does excuse),
and I—with her—evacuated...
How often did my tender muse
relieve the passing territory
by charming with a secret story!
How often a Caucasian bluff,
beneath the moon, we'd gallop rough!
How often to Crimean beaches
in nighttime gloom she'd quickly bound
to hear the ceaseless seaside sound,
a nereid's soft whispered speeches,
the rollers' deep, eternal choir,
a paean to the planet's sire.

8.V
With the far capital forgotten—
both splendor and each noisy fête—
she visits, in the misbegotten
Moldavia (rhyme's epithet!),
plain tents of a nomadic nation,

and lost in them domestication,
and there gave up the words of God
for tongues both limited and odd,
for songs about the steppe (the poem
our Pushkin wrote, she'd venerate)...
When all became—poof!—his estate
and suddenly she changed to show him
a country miss with thoughtful look
and in her hands a small French book.

8.VI
His exile done, he's gratifying
his muse with her premier soirée.
I watch, he writes, with jealous shying
at steppe-land charm now on display.
Through serried ranks of dignitaries,
of army fops and emissaries,
past proud ladies, her feet near glide.
She sits serene to watch wide-eyed
the noisy crush with admiration,
and flashing dresses and the prate,
and sluggish guests appearing late
(to the young hostess's vexation),
and rings of gentlemen dark dressed,
the frames for ladies at their best.

8.VII
(How I adore this verse transition,
where Pushkin's art's a seamless glide!)
My muse enjoys the composition
of conversation stratified.
The cold of quiet pride engages
and, too, the mix of rank and ages.
But who's this in the chosen throng,
obscure and mute? Does he belong?
Before him flash the line of faces
as tiresome specters. Is it spleen
or pained conceit upon his mien?

Why is he here? Why—of all places—
is that Eugene?... "Well, you're not wrong."
"Tell me, has he been back for long?

8.VIII
And has he changed? Domesticated?
(The question fits Nadezhda, too.
What's new since I evacuated?)
Does he still act a touch askew?
Do tell, who was he on returning?
Who is he now? A foreign-yearning
sophisticate, a slavophile,
Childe Harold, Quaker, something vile?
Flaunts he another mask? Or will he
be simply good, like you or me—
like all of our society?
But my advice: give up the really
outdated roles. Enough. They're so..."
"You know him then?" "Well, yes and no."

8.IX
"Then why are you so damned begrudging?
Is it because we never shrug
from busying ourselves in judging
most everything? Because the smug
nobody finds the fervid spirit
offensive or absurd? Or here it
is wit that's getting in your face?
Or we're too eager to embrace
chatter in place of facts? That folly
is simply frivolous and cruel?
(So Pushkin obfuscates the duel.
Eugene's the one maligned, by golly!)
Or is the commonplace alone
just who we are, all we condone?"

8.X
Yes, Pushkin here rewrites his story.

The blest were youthful in their youth.
And blest were those matured in season,
who learned to tolerate life's freeze in
each passing year, didn't pursue
their strangest dreams, didn't eschew
the social mob, who were at twenty
a fop or blade, at thirty wed,
at fifty years, out of the red,
whose fame and ranks and money (plenty!)
arrived with ease in turn, and who
were called *first rate* their life all through.

8.XI
But it is sad to think of how our
fleet youth was given us in vain,
how we betrayed it every hour,
how it deceived us with disdain,
that each magnificent desire
and that our freshest dreams entire
did quickly decompose in turn,
as leaves in rainy autumn's churn.
And it's too much to see before us
a single meal night after night,
to look on life as on a rite,
to follow in decorum's chorus
and never share the public view
nor they the passions we pursue.

8.XII
Having become a goss sensation,
it is past bearing (you'll agree)
to have—midst prigs—the reputation
of an unhappy oddity
or pseudo crank, satanic devil
or my own "Demon." (Pushkin's revel
that blurs again the line between

And speaking of: why, after sending
his dearest friend across the Styx,
he'd lazed till he was twenty-six.
And languishing in never-ending
repose, without a post or wife,
he'd found no purpose to his life.

8.XIII
Overtaken by agitation,
he wanted then a change of scene.

He left his grounds, secluded green,
the forests that had daily taunted
with Lensky's bloodied shade. Thus haunted,
he started wandering without aim,
which his emotions then became.
As with all that his set had offered,
his travels, too, grew tiresome.

Eugene returned to take a fall
straight from a ship into a ball.

8.XIV
A ripple through the throng was spreading,
a whisper racing through the lull,
for to the hostess there was heading
a lady with her general.
She was not rushed, not cold nor gushing,
without an imitative blushing,
without an impudent noblesse,
without a pretense to success,
without those little mannerisms...
For all in her was quiet, clear.
A portrait true did she appear
du comme il faut...

8.XV

Now towards her were ladies fetching,
and the old women smiled her way.
The men bowed low, with hopes of catching
her glancing eye, while girls would stray
in rustling view. With nose and shoulders
held higher than her keen beholders
was her escorting general.
None could have called her beautiful.
From head down to her foot, however,
not one could have obtained therein
what autocratic fashion in
the highest London sets whatever
calls, "vulgar." (Pushkin wrote this word
in English. Translate? He demurred...)

8.XVI

"I cannot," Pushkin wrote, and neither
can I. This narrative's not mine.
Eugene is not Nadezhda's either,
although she breathes beyond this line,
in parallels through this creation,
in Pushkin's dearest adoration...
This poem shows life's pantheon.
Beneath the garland... is she gone?
No. No, she's right. My motivations
are Pushkin's selfish saboteurs.
This isn't mine, it isn't hers,
and she won't hear "congratulations."
I should step back, you will agree,
if vulgar I don't want to be.

* Our bard's true verse is explanation:
  I very much adore this word,
  but I can give you no translation.
  For us it's new but scarce preferred
  (now "vulgar" is in Russian rooted),
  back then an epigram would suit it...
  Returning to our unnamed dear,
  with carefree charm, she's seated near
  a fiction, Nina Voronskaya,
  the sparkling Cleopatra on
  the Neva. The debate's forgone:
  the unnamed's charm would sure belie a
  conceit that marble beauty could
  eclipse with dazzle over good.

8.XVII
"Well!" thinks the hero of our novel.
"Could it be her? But really... No...
How? From a backwoods village hovel..."
And his obsessed lorgnette will go
to her whose air recalls—obscurely—
the face forgotten prematurely.
"Now don't you know, prince... Can you say
who's in that raspberry beret,
the woman talking with the Spanish
ambassador?" The nameless prince
stares at Onegin. "Oh! Well, since
so long ago you did quite vanish—
Just wait. I'll introduce you two."
"But who is she?" "My wife, that's who."

8.XVIII
"I didn't know! When did you marry?"
"Around two years ago." "To who?"
"The Larin girl." "Extraordinary!
Tatiana!" "Ah, you know her, too?"
"We're country neighbors." (Pushkin's vague in
what he reveals about Onegin,
whose questions feel they're skirting dread
—as Tanya mourned when Olga wed).
Now to his wife the prince is leading.
Tatiana peers upon this wight...
Within her soul, whatever fright,
whatever shame it was succeeding,
her tone betrayed nothing. Somehow
she kept the quiet of her bow.

8.XIV
It's not just that she never shuddered
nor turned abruptly flush or white...
Her brow not once so much as fluttered,
nor did her lip so much as bite.
Although regarding her intently,

Onegin couldn't consequently
detect a trace of who she'd been.
He wished discussion would begin
but nope—he couldn't. She, though, queried.
She asked when he'd returned, and whence,
of home, and if he'd traveled hence.
Then to her spouse she turned her wearied
attention. And she slipped away...
But there, quite still, Eugene did stay.

8.XX
Was she the same—was he mistaken?—
this Tanya from our novel's start,
the one he'd met in parts forsaken?
Was this the same innocent heart
he'd one time lectured, patronizing
with righteous, ardent moralizing,
whose letter he preserved as yet
(and passed to Pushkin, don't forget!),
the letter where that heart's in writing,
where all is plain and all extreme,
that little girl... Was this a dream?...
That little girl, whom he'd scorned, slighting
her humble lot, was she just there,
so bold, so distant in her air?

8.XXI
He leaves the wall-to-wall reception,
rides brooding home, where arrant dreams
disturb his sleep (in the conception
that characters are wed by themes).
He wakes with a communication.
Prince X has sent an invitation
to a soirée. "My God! To her!...
Oh, yes, I will!" Without defer,
he scribbles out his approbation.
How strange he is! What dream has sway?
What stirred the depths to so dismay

a cold and languid soul? Vexation?
Conceit? Or a resurgence of
that adolescent trouble—love?

8.XXII
Once more Onegin counts each hour,
awaiting the day's end—once more.
But it is striking ten, and now our
Eugene leaves, flies, is at the door.
He enters, trembling, seeks the splendid,
and finds Tatiana unattended.
For several minutes, the two sit
together. (Awkwardnesses split
the lines in Russian.) Words not daring
Onegin's lips, morose and tense,
he hardly answers her. His sense
strains with tenacious thought. He's staring
most stubbornly at her, while she
is sitting peacefully and free.

8.XXIII
Her husband then, with his arrival,
breaks up this dreadful tête-à-tête.
The prince remembers with his rival
the jokes and japes of their old set.
They laugh. The guests begin arriving.
The conversation started thriving
with the coarse salt of social hate.
Before the hostess, easy prate
flowed without foolish affectation,
and, meanwhile, interrupting it
was decent talk without foul wit,
eternal truth, or pedantation.
It didn't shock a single ear
with its relaxed but lively cheer.

8.XXIV
Imagination goes wherever,

and Pushkin flirted with the pull
of Tanya. Truth describes, however,
the flower of the capital:
nobility and fashion's graces,
essential fools, familiar faces.
Here were old dames, in cap and rose,
with wicked airs. Where were the beaux?
Here was a lone, unsmiling maiden.
Here was an envoy now abuzz
with government affairs, and 'twas
a gray-head, smelling of pomade, in
the midst of telling an old joke—
he's subtle, smart, but hardly woke.

8.XXV
Here was a gentleman. Delighted
by epigrams, he cursed the rest:
the party's tea (that sugar blighted),
trite ladies' thoughts, how men impressed,
a boring novel's dull debating,
two sisters made ladies-in-waiting,
newspapers' lies, some foreign strife,
the snow, and, clearly, his own wife.
Here lines were cut in Pushkin's battle
to get the party "right." His plume
described a hunchbacked puppet, whom
Nabokov calls—while hating tattle—
an unrequited love. The proof?
She had a lithe and little hoof.

8.XXVI
Here was the social climber, noted
for the debasement of his soul,
whom sketchist Count St.-Priest devoted
albums of pencil lead to troll.
Another ballroom despot's posing
in the doorway: tight suit exposing,
and cherub pink with frozen mien,

mute as a fashion magazine.
Here—like Eugene, if we're comparing—
an unexpected traveler:
this over-starched and shameless sir
brought smiles with his deliberate bearing.
And with a silent, passing look,
the public judged him crank or crook.

8.XXVII
But the whole eve Eugene fixated
on dear Tatiana all alone,
not on the girl so twitterpated,
so shy, sincere, her feelings known,
but on the princess who's so chilly,
the distant goddess of the really
ornate and regal Neva. Oh,
poor Pushkin cut a splendid show
of Nina, the set's Prima Donna,
who was with burning diamonds crowned,
with patterned silk, unfurling, gowned,
and who—long last—eclipsed Tatiana.
Instead, he talks of Eve, the snake,
how paradise must have the ache.

8.XXVIII
Behold Tatiana's transformation!
How thoroughly she took her role!
How quick was Tanya's acclimation
to such a stiffening of soul!
Who'd dare to seek the tender maiden
in the majestic calm displayed in
this arbiter of parlor grace?
He'd held her heart in his embrace!
For him she'd spend the darkness pining,
while Morpheus had yet to light,
and lift her languid, virgin sight
to the fair moon, so gently shining,
and dream of sometime, as his wife,
faring the humble road of life!

8.XXIX
All ages are to love submissive,
but to our young and virgin hearts,
the ageist Pushkin's more permissive
and says her surges play their parts:
Like storms in vernal fields, a shower
of passion will rouse, ripen, flower—
and potent life gives hecatombs
of fragrant fruit and splendid blooms.
But in the late and fruitless ages,
but when our years turn in their course,
a dying passion brings remorse,
as frigid autumn's rainstorm rages
to inundate a meadow's share
and strip the nearby forest bare.

8.XXX
There is no doubt. Alas! Eugene is
in love with Tanya like a child.
In yearning, he passes between his
long nights and days with love run wild.
Not heeding common sense reproaches,
his carriage every day approaches
her glassed foyer and colonnade.
Eugene pursues her like a shade.
And he is happy if he's bundling
her shoulders in a sable snake
or if he heatedly can take
her hand or—better—if he's trundling
her through the colors of a ball
or even picking up her shawl.

8.XXXI
She doesn't notice him. (Reprising,
this Pushkin wrote when Tanya bared
her heart and missed the sun's arising.
Now it's Eugene's that's near declared.)
At home, Tatiana's free in greeting,

while out, three words, a bow at meeting,
or sometimes she just doesn't stop.
But coquetry she lacks a drop—
society does not permit it
(and thus we know it's fiction). So
Eugene grows pale. She doesn't know—
or doesn't care. He pines, committed.
All send doctors, whose common will
send him to waters—and a bill.

8.XXXII
He does not go. He's nearly writing
his ancestors they'll meet betime.
This isn't Tanya's business. (Slighting
all women, Pushkin gets his rhyme
and blames her sex.) Eugene is mulish.
He won't give up. He hopes. (He's foolish.)
Bold as a healthy firebrand,
the sick man writes, though weak of hand,
the princess an impassioned missive
(despite his noting in the main
but scant in letters not in vain).
To heartfelt hurt he was submissive
(although, like Tanya, first demurred),
so here's his letter, word for word.

8. Onegin's Letter to Tatiana

          I see it all: perceived dispraise
at this sad secret's explanation,
and such a bitter indignation
expressed by your disdainful gaze.
But why? What am I going after
in opening my soul to you?
To what malicious fun and laughter
will I, perhaps, thus give the cue?

By chance, we'd met. You were appealing,
and glimmerings of your fine feeling
had dared me to believe. But no.
This sweet habit I'd not engender.
I hadn't wanted to surrender
my hateful freedom. Then a blow
divided us...Poor Lensky's dying
was an unlucky sacrifice...
From all that's dear—it's mortifying—
I tore my heart from paradise.
I was a stranger in migration.
Freedom and peace, I did profess
a substitute for happiness.
What a mistake, what a damnation!

        No, constantly to see your face,
to follow you all over, catching
with loving eyes the smiling grace
upon your lips, your eyes so fetching,
to pay attention long and grasp
within my soul your perfect measure,
to ache before you, then to gasp,
to pale and fade... Now this is pleasure!

        And I'm deprived of this. For you,
I drag myself here, there. I wander.
My days are few, my hours, too,
but I—in futile boredom—squander
the days once counted off by fate.
And now they are a painful weight.
I know its measure has been taken,
but to prolong my mortal stay,
I must be sure when I awaken
that I will meet with you that day...

        I fear that in my humble pleading
your scathing glances will discern
a stratagem of vile misleading—

that you will in your anger spurn.
And if you knew but how abhorrent
it is to languish in love's thirst,
to blaze—and hourly calm the torrent
within your blood by thoughts coerced,
to wish to ever be enfolding
your knees and, sobbing at your feet,
to pour out pleas, confessions, scolding,
and every word that could entreat,
the while to arm both speech and bearing
with such a fraudulent sangfroid,
then comfortably and calmly jaw
and gaily take you in with staring!...

        But so it is. I'm in no state
to stay myself. That's my confession.
Now all's resolved. At your discretion,
I give myself up to my fate.

8.XXXIII
There's no reply. He sends a second,
a third—and nothing. (Added late,
the letter's style. First Pushkin reckoned
these gaps we could extrapolate.)
Eugene goes out to a reception...
She draws near, scathing in perception!
He isn't seen. No word is told.
She's cloaked in epiphanic cold!
How stubborn lips strain at concealing
her indignation! Long he stares
with penetrating sight. Where... Where's
her disarray, her fellow feeling?
Where marks of tears? No sign! This face
displays—and just—her anger's trace...

8.XXXIV
...or, maybe, secret consternation
lest husband or society

should guess the ruse, the chance temptation...
All my Onegin could quite see...
There is no hope! (This fear rehearses
within my thoughts.) He leaves and curses
his folly—and, plunged deep within,
renounced society again.
And in his study's endless quiet,
he could recall that time and place,
when melancholy's gloom would chase
him through the endless social riot,
when it would catch, by collar seize,
lock him away, and toss the keys.

8.XXXV
Again he read without discernment.
He read Rousseau and Gibbon, too.
He read de Staël without adjournment.
And Pushkin lists—as he will do—
those of forgotten reputation.
Nabokov starts an estimation
of time Eugene spent reading—then
abandons it. Who cares? *Again*,
it's fiction, yet Onegin could've
perused first excerpts of *Eugene*
in journals, almanacs he'd seen,
where, Pushkin notes: He often would've
met madrigals that smeared me then—
e sempre bene, gentlemen.

8.XXXVI
And what? Onegin's eyes were reading,
but then his thoughts so distant stole.
His dreams, desires, griefs exceeding
were crowding deeply in his soul.
Within the printed lines' division,
he read with spiritual vision
quite other words. In lines unversed,
Eugene was utterly immersed.

They were legends, the secret fictions
of hazy bygones of the heart,
the dreams that breathed alone, apart,
the threats, the talk, the vague predictions,
or lengthy stories' liveliness,
or letters from a youthful miss.

8.XXXVII
And he slow slumps into cessation
of both senses and thoughts' demand.
Before him, then, imagination
casts down her motley faro hand.
And now he sees, as if there sleeping
on melting snow, a youth there keeping
so motionless, so still, so dread.
He hears a voice. "Looks like...he's dead."
And now he sees forgotten rivals,
and vile poltroons and slandering churls,
a swarm of young, unfaithful girls,
and loathsome comrades' mean arrivals,
and now the country house—and see!
She's at the window...always she!...

8.XXXVIII
With dreams and shadows, Pushkin's twining
the altered themes thought left behind.
Onegin took to his declining
so much he all but lost his mind—
or turned poet. (A consummation
devoutly to be wished!) Translation:
through magnetism's steady draw,
my addled pupil nearly saw
the movement of our Russian verses.
How like a poet, when he'd face
the lonely, burning fireplace.
The corner his, he hums, rehearses
a gondolier's romance, and to
the flame yields journal or a shoe.

8.XXXIX
Days rushed along. Already winter
resolved in the warm air. And he
did not turn poet (here I enter),
nor did he die, nor go *crazeee*.
The spring revived him. Long awaited,
his locked rooms (where he'd hibernated,
just like a marmot), inglenook,
his double windows, all he took
initial leave one sunny morning.
He skims the Neva in a sleigh.
On hewn blue blocks of ice, the spray
of sunlight plays. On streets adorning
is dirty, upturned, melting snow.
And where with such a speedy show

8.XL
does my Eugene direct his bearing?
You've guessed already. Truly. My
incorrigible crank came tearing
to her, to his Tatiana. Why,
he's like a dead man (almost dreaming).
The entrance should in truth be teeming.
There's not a soul. An empty hall,
a door, and then what should enthrall?
The princess now before him, sitting,
both pale and unadorned, alone.
She had been reading what's not shown—
some letter Pushkin's art finds fitting
to hint is *his*. She's quiet, meek,
and cries, while leaning, hand on cheek.

8.XLI
Who could not read her silent anguish
in this quick instant! Who could not
discern the former Tanya languish
within the princess here distraught!
With mad regrets and aching-hearted,

Eugene fell at her feet. She started
and silently looks in his eyes
with neither anger nor surprise...
Onegin's ailing, spent impression,
his mute reproach, his pleading mien:
to our Tatiana, all are seen.
The country girl of plain expression,
with dreams and heart of bygone years,
now stirs in her and reappears.

8.XLII
She doesn't bid him rise, nor turning
her eyes from his, does she withdraw
her heartless hand from lips so yearning...
Within Onegin, Pushkin saw
Tatiana from afar. What's passing
within her reverie? Amassing
time passes long in silence, and
at last, she, softly: "Enough. Stand.
I should explain to you directly.
Onegin, please recall the day—
that hour along the park's allée,
where fate had brought us, and abjectly
I listened as you lectured me?
Today is mine—my turn, you see.

8.XLIII
"Then I was younger—and more pretty,
at least, Onegin, to my mind.
I did love you. Oh, what a pity.
Within your heart what did I find?
How'd you respond to me? Severely.
Is this not true? Did you then merely
find shy young love already old?
And now—goodness, gracious!—how cold
my blood runs to recall your dour
expression and that homily...
But I don't blame you: towards me,

you were correct that awful hour.
You acted with a noble goal.
And I'm obliged with all my soul...

8.XLIV
"Back then, off in the godforsaken,
far from vain talk, it's true that you
did not like me... Why are you taken
with me now? Why do you pursue
me? Is it not because my station
now has a social obligation
and I'm in high society?
Because I'm rich nobility?
Because my husband was in battle
maimed, thus is blessed with courtly fame?
And is it not because my shame
would be remarked with endless tattle
within our set and would reflect
on you a scandalous respect?

8.XLV
"I'm crying...if you've not forgotten
your Tanya yet, then know: your cold,
strict conversation, being caught in
the sharp rebuking of your scold—
if it was only in my power,
I'd have preferred that life, your glower,
to vulgar lusts, these letters, tears.
If you'd accounted for my years
or demonstrated some compassion
for girlish, guileless dreams... But now!
What reason could compel you bow
just at my feet? What trifling passion!
How could your heart and mind withal
become a petty feeling's thrall?

8.XLVI
"To me, Onegin, these excesses,

the tchotchkes of these hateful days,
my social whirlwind's 'grand' successes,
my stylish house and my soirées,
are all for what? I'd gladly render
all this elation, noise, and splendor,
the tatters of this masquerade,
for shelves of books and garden shade,
for our poor home and sanctuary,
those places where, by lucky chance,
Onegin, I'd first met your glance,
and for the humble cemetery,
where now a cross and tree converse
above my poor and dearest nurse...

8.XLVII
"This happiness was near decided.
It was so close!... But fate, my years
are otherwise resolved. Misguided,
perhaps, I acted so. Through tears
of prayer, my mother pleaded, stressing
that every lot was here a blessing
for her poor Tanya... I made good,
I did get married. And you should,
I beg, leave me. I know, however,
within your heart there does abide
a proper honor next to pride.
I love you (why should I be clever?),
but I am now another's wife
and will be faithful all my life."

8.XLVIII
She exited. Eugene is reeling.
His heart is deep immersed—near drowned—
in such a thunderstorm of feeling!
But with the (long-expected) sound,
the spurs and Tanya's husband enter
(and Eugene wakes from his long winter).
And here, dear reader, Pushkin writes,

as this unpleasant moment lights
on him, my hero we'll abandon
for long... for ever. After him
we wandered long enough by whim
through Russia's world. Let us disband and
part from the shore (perhaps the strand
where Pushkin missed his fathers' land).

8.XLIX
Now then, o reader mine, whoever
you may be, whether friend or foe,
when we do say goodbye forever,
I want you as a friend. And so,
whatever in these careless verses
you sought from me, be they sharp curses,
or stormy memoirs, living scenes,
or holidays from work routines,
or flaws in grammar (or translation),
God grant that in this book you've found
if but an ounce—if not a pound—
for daydreams or for recreation,
for journals' brawls, or for the heart.
With this, goodbye! Now let us part.

8.L
Goodbye to my strange friend in touring,
to you, my true ideal, adieu,
and you, my living and enduring,
but little, work, farewell. With you,
I've tasted all a poet's yearning:
the vacant life of social churning
and charming talks with friends I've known.
And many, many days have flown
since first, in dim imagination,
the juvenile Tatiana dear
with my Onegin did appear—
back then this novel's liberation,
regarded through a crystal ball,
I scarcely could discern at all.

8.LI
But at a meeting of my brothers,
to whom I read the opening first...
"Already some are not, and others
are far away," as Saadi versed.
(Decembrists lost to death or jailing.
In this, *my* government is failing...)
Without them all, Onegin's drawn,
and dear Tatiana's model's... (gone)
Fate's added many to its tally!
Thus blest is one who early flees
life's feast, not drinking to the lees,
who hasn't read through life's finale
and learned how one just leaves a friend,
as I must now Eugene. The end.

Alexander Sergeyevich Pushkin (1799-1837) is considered to be Russia's greatest poet and the father of modern Russian literature. Born into Russian nobility in Moscow, the great-grandson of Peter the Great's African godson Ibrahim Hannibal, he published his first poem at age 15 and quickly won acclaim amongst the literati. Following the circulation of "Ode to Liberty" (among other poems), he was exiled to what is now Moldova and southern Ukraine in 1820. He began writing the novel in verse *Eugene Onegin* three years into his exile, from which he was released by the death of Czar Alexander I in 1825. Pushkin subsequently remained under watch in Russia's capitals and there published *Onegin* in serial form. The long poem *Ruslan and Ludmila*, the short story "The Captain's Daughter," and the play *Boris Godunov*, among many other stories, plays, and poems, complete the body of his work. Always a proud, irascible man, Pushkin was mortally wounded in a duel with the rumored lover of his wife.

Robert E. Tanner was educated in New Orleans, Paris, and New York and served in the Peace Corps in Ukraine from 2018 to 2020. He began translating *Eugene Onegin* in Mykolaiv, Ukraine, as part of the Peace Corps' Third Goal ("to help promote a better understanding of other peoples on the part of Americans"), and finished his translation in the United States during the pandemic lockdowns of 2020-2021. His writing has appeared in *Blue Unicorn*, *The New Orleans Review*, *The Brooklyn Rail*, *The Collagist*, *The Quarterly Conversation*, and in other places. He is neither particularly proud nor remarkably irascible, but a fatal duel is not off the table.